PARDS OF
BUFFALO BILL

TOM CURRY

SAGEBRUSH
Large Print Westerns

First published in the United States by Curtis Books

First Isis Edition
published 2018
by arrangement with
Golden West Literary Agency

A catalogue record for this book is available
from the British Library.

ISBN 978–1–78541–557–9 (pb)

Published by
F. A. Thorpe (Publishing)
Anstey, Leicestershire

Set by Words & Graphics Ltd.
Anstey, Leicestershire
Printed and bound in Great Britain by
T. J. International Ltd., Padstow, Cornwall

This book is printed on acid-free paper

CHAPTER
ONE

Hades Comes on Wheels

The string of flatcars screeched to a stop at the raw end of the new railroad tracks, slowly but surely crawling westward toward the Pacific. The Union Pacific was building, after the Civil War, and the madness of speculation, of overnight fortunes, gripped the swiftly expanding Nation, released from the horror of internecine conflict.

"Junction City!" howled a bearded brakeman, and laborers began throwing off the makings of entire buildings. When fitted together they would make up the town's larger structures, such as all-important saloons. Bars, boxes, bales, barrels, tools, tents, lumber sailed off, impelled by the brawny arms of graders and track-layers, so that the workers and those who battened upon them might be housed, fed and entertained while the portable city remained on that particular spot in the vast Nebraska plains. In what seemed the twinkling of an eye hundreds of hands had erected a rip-snorting Frontier camp of raw boards and canvas. Saloons, dance-halls and gambling palaces were surprisingly large.

In short order they were jammed with sweated humanity as the workmen tossed away their hard-earned money.

Junction City would be their metropolis for weeks, depending on the progress made in building the track, an average of two miles per day.

It was not yet dark when "Gentleman Dan" Kane, in a black broadcloth suit and fine leather boots stood in the door of his own place.

It was a good-sized shack having a large tent annex for use as a gambling hall and bar.

Kane was tall and wide of shoulder. He was a trained boxer and quick with his hands, an asset in his profession — the manipulation of cards.

There was a contemptuous curl to Gentleman Dan's thin-lipped mouth, adorned by a silky black mustache. His crisp dark hair curled down around his ears, one of which was well formed while the other had been cauliflowered, the memento of a prizefight. For, when younger, he had actually believed in toiling for his money.

"Tex," Kane called, flicking an inch of gray ash from his West Indian cheroot, "have you seen those clodhoppers?"

A big lobster-complexioned man in leather, and wearing a wide Stetson, swung over. His hair was bleached, he had a massive jaw, a broken nose, and a wide gap where three front teeth had been rammed down his throat by a rifle butt.

"Nope, Dan," he replied. "But I'm still a-watchin' for 'em."

"Take a walk up to the other end of the camp," ordered Kane. "They may be there."

2

The man nodded, and obediently waddled off with the bowlegged gait of a cowboy.

"Tex" O'Byrne had been a ranch hand. He had come up the Jones and Plummer Trail from the Lone Star State with a herd after the War. But his heart was not in ranch work, for in that heart was room only for a burning hate and a desire for revenge.

He had never been a soldier in the Confederate ranks, but a guerrilla raider in Quantrell's murderous band. Once Federal troops, a cavalry detachment, had surprised him and his mates as they burned a victim's home, and Tex was still bitter about the wound he had received in escaping. A rope would have been his lot had he been captured.

After a time, Tex came ambling back, with three men in tow. They were middle-aged, decent looking fellows with the reddened, calloused hands of hard-working men.

"Here's Mr. Kane, gents," drawled O'Byrne. "Yuh kin palaver with him."

"Come in, will you, please?" asked Gentleman Dan smoothly.

The trio trailed him into the shack, with some reluctance. All wore homespun garments, rough, muddy riding boots and flat hats.

Their leader was around forty-five, his curly brown hair just touched with gray at the temples. His skin was rugged, and determined, and his dark-gray eyes dauntless. The broad, firm mouth, lined at the corners, showed capacity for compassion as well as fighting

3

strength. This man had suffered, and had won out against odds.

"I'm James Barringer," he told Kane. "What did yuh want to see me about?"

"Sit down, please," said Gentleman Dan, waving hospitably at the full bottle of whiskey on the table.

"Help yourselves," he invited graciously.

One of Barringer's companions reached for the bottle, but at a quick frown from his friend, he waited. Kane pretended not to notice.

"I have important business to discuss with you," he said in his well modulated voice. "Barringer, you own the Slanting B Ranch on the Wood River?"

"I can't deny that," replied Barringer dryly.

"Then listen carefully," continued Kane, ignoring the obvious coldness of the men, "for it means a vast fortune to you and to me — oh, all perfectly honest and above-board, though I'll beg you to treat what we say here as strictly confidential. Lewis Miller, you own a section in Riverside, your town. John Ulman, you hold land along the Wood."

He placed one hand inside his ruffled white shirt front, a look of importance on his face.

"Do you, Barringer," he asked impressively, "believe that the railroad is going to strike near your land, and that it will make an important stop of your settlement, Riverside?"

"We shore thought so," Barringer said softly. "The engineers surveyed through our town, and they hinted to us the U.P. might locate shops there. The river's good water."

4

"Yes, and a big flow," agreed Kane. "However, gents, I have means of gaining information denied to you. That survey was a fake, to prevent folks from gaining control over too much land near the U.P.'s real right-of-way. The real roadbed will be graded thirty miles south. Anyway, it'll be next summer before the graders reach the Wood River. Winter's coming on."

"And what's all this mean to us?" asked Barringer.

"Isn't it plain, sir? Your land won't be worth anything like it would be if you settled on the actual route. Here's my proposition. We form the Western Nebraska Land Company, all of us putting up equal money for control."

"We ain't got any money," Barringer growled, turned away.

"Wait! I'll put up cash. You fellows can sell your present holdings and get your friends to transfer to the new site. We'll clean up millions!"

A derisive smile tooched Barringer's strong mouth.

"Not interested," he said, turning away again.

The polished surface rubbed off Gentleman Dan Kane for a moment. He seized Barringer's sleeve and stopped him.

"Wait a jiffy, Barringer. What's the matter? You treat me like I was scum."

"You are," snapped Barringer. "Take yore paw off me, Kane. I savvy you. In the first place, I ain't tryin' to make a fortune on a gamble. I love my home and mean to keep it, railroad or no railroad. In the second, if I was huntin' a deal, I wouldn't go pardners with a crook."

Kane's face flushed. His fists clenched but, glancing at the three powerful frontiersmen, he changed his mind and shrugged. Violence was repugnant to him, actually.

When Barringer and his two friends had gone, Kane opened a small side panel leading into a semi-dark sleeping cubicle. A man sat there on the bunk, his eyes glowing red.

"You heard them, Boss," growled Kane. "The yokels!"

"Barringer's the chief stumbling-block, Kane. He's shrewd and leery, stubborn as an old mule. He's holding the rest and has warned Miller and Ulman now. They can't go home, that's all. I'll wipe out the whole bunch of 'em if need be."

Kane drew in a sharp breath, and the man called "Boss" glanced at him quickly. The gambler, who did not find it too great a stretch of conscience to cheat, had an aversion to killing.

"Is it necessary to kill them, Boss?" he asked. "Why not just —"

The Boss seized his wrist, glaring.

"You're small-time, Kane! I'm giving you a big chance and you hem and haw. Don't be a yellow fool. You're with me, aren't you?"

Kane was rattled. "Oh, yeah, sure."

"Then dry up and travel the road I show you. I'll tell Tex what to do. I mean to connect with Spotted Tail of the Brule Sioux as soon as possible. And when I tell you to do a job, go to it."

Kane promised. He seized the bottle, and took a stiff drink.

Tex O'Byrne, who did not share Kane's dislike of blood-letting, received his orders. Two days later he waited with his men, hidden in one of the numerous dry ravines which split the vast, short-grassed Nebraska plains. Save along the rivers where there were timber belts, and occasional prairie groves, the plains stretched in every direction. Over them were run the food, clothing, fuel, housing material supply of the Indians. And here buffalo ranged.

O'Byrne had made a swift ride to get ahead of Barringer and his two friends, Miller and Ulman, whose arrival he now awaited with deep relish. He had grown to enjoy bloodshed during his runs with Quantrell.

The gang he had formed at Junction City, over a hundred miles back eastward, and of which these men with him were a part, was composed of assorted cutthroats from every corner of the globe, including murderers from the dives of Marseille and Hamburg, from Africa, and from the lands to the south of the growing United States.

It was easy to assemble such a bunch. A bottle of red-eye, a horse and gun, a dollar or two, besides what loot they picked up, made up their pay. Most of them had come out to work on the railroad and had found it too much like work. Others were frankly on the dodge, ready for criminal connections.

"There they come, boys," grunted Tex, to his dozen rowdies, whose saddled horses were waiting in the hidden ravine. "Whoop it up and we'll drop a couple eagle feathers and carve the Sioux mark on the bodies. Don't let any get away now!"

Indian feathers were stuck in coarse hair that was tied back by bandannas, and blankets were draped about brawny shoulders. It was a common dodge to dress like savages when such affairs were afoot.

Jim Barringer and his two friends came riding along, headed for their home on the western border of Nebraska. They would pass within a few hundred yards of the ravine, following the easier contour of the land ocean. To the naked eye, the plains seemed empty for mile after mile, with nothing in sight save the distant dots of buffalo.

Tex O'Byrne had a rifle with special sights. He leveled it as he crouched, and pulled the trigger. Barringer was hit in the side, and he slumped, not dead but seriously wounded.

"Up and at 'em!" bellowed Tex.

The gang rode from the ravine, quirting their horses. Wild whoops and curses rang out. A volley hit Miller's horse broadside and sent it sprawling. Ulman shot back at the attackers. He hit one, who fell out of line, but revolvers and carbines concentrated on him as he rode off at a swift clip.

Lewis Miller was dismounted, and Barringer, still able to stay on his saddle, brought his big black back to his comrade, hoping to pick Miller up and save him. But Tex O'Byrne and his men came on, their guns roaring fast.

8

More lead drove into Miller and Barringer as they started away. The black mustang, hit in a dozen places, slowly sank to the plain.

Neither Miller nor Barringer could get up, although Barringer did push up on one elbow, and fire a bullet that whizzed close to Tex's ear. The big killer banged away in fury. Barringer was bleeding from many wounds, and his arm fell. But O'Byrne, in a bloody rage, leaped from his horse and jumped on the prostrate man's face, smashing it in with his heavy, iron-shod boots.

He emptied his six-shooter into Barringer's body, shrieking curses as he ground the man's features under his heel. Ejecting the empty shells, he reloaded and fired three more shots into Barringer, who was already gone. Others of the gunmen had finished off Miller, and Tex, nostrils flared with blood lust, eyes blazing, jumped on his saddle and spurred after John Ulman who, seeing that his friends were hopelessly done for, was racing for his own life.

At a mad pace they tore across the rolling plains. In the distance the buffalo raised massive, shaggy heads, nervously sniffing.

Riding fresh horses, Tex and his mates easily overtook Ulman. They left him dead in the grass, his head a bloody horror with the scalp slashed off. His pockets and saddle-bags were rifled a la Sioux.

It was far from being the first human blood these great plains had thirstily drunk up. For the California Trail ran near here and the bleached bones of men, women and their children nestled in the curling grass, victims of savages, starvation and icy blizzards.

Through here, along the line of the Platte, the Mormon battalions had struggled, some pushing hand carts through the fifteen hundred miles of wilderness to reach Zion. Gold-seekers, buffalo hunters, explorers, men on the dodge had passed through here, side by side with holy men carrying the torch into the wilds, and the best people of the States.

Emigrants had come from every land. Pony express riders, freighters, stage-coachers, writers and engineers, soldiers on the march of conquest and pacification, had passed along the Platte, a "mile wide and an inch deep," on that tremendous trek of Mankind, ever pushing west.

O'Byrne glanced toward where the Platte gleamed some miles off, and the Overland Trail ran. He took a swig of whiskey from a flask and passed it around, his blood-lust sated for a moment.

"The Boss says there'll be plenty more later, boys," he remarked, his flat nostrils flared with the salty tang of gore. "And plenty in it for them who ride our trail."

CHAPTER
TWO

Emigrant Train

Young Jim Barringer pushed his buckskin at a swift clip over the plains.

His father was overdue at home at the Slanting B, and Jim, named for his dad, had come to hunt him.

He was a stalwart young fellow of twenty, with the same frank, dark gray eyes and curly brown hair of his parent. His broad-shouldered youthful body was clad in fringed buckskin. His riding boots had large-roweled silver spurs, and he wore a flat-crowned "Nebraska" hat, strapped to his firm, bronzed jaw.

His features were pleasantly symmetrical, and he had no beard or mustache, but his mouth showed determination and he was alert, as all trained plainsmen had to be. A loaded .50 caliber Sharps buffalo gun rested across his pommel and two loaded pistols were in his belt.

"Bucky," he suddenly complained to his mount, "what ails yuh?"

Bucky, as fast as a wind gust, sniffed uneasily, dancing a bit.

Young Barringer, who did a good deal of hunting buffalo, selling the hides and supplying the neighbors with beef, a job which he preferred to working on his father's ranch, was a trained, born plainsman. His keen eyes searching now, to discover what had disturbed his sensitive horse, rested on the slight difference in shade where the ravine cut emerged to the surface of the curling grass.

But off to his left something gray, and then more like it, slunk off at his approach, and black objects whirred into the air.

Flowers bedecked the ground, growing amidst the dense buffalo grass, and the autumn day was mellow and warm with the brilliant sun. It was as bland as honey, giving no hint of tragedy, any more than it suggested that killing, icy blasts of winter swept those same plains. All seemed at peace, gently beautiful.

Jim Barringer allowed Bucky to edge off from the shaded patch, which marked one of the numerous splits in the flatlands, and which the Sioux used as hiding-places from which to ambush unsuspecting travelers. Indians were notoriously poor shots, though, and Bucky, who had Arab blood in him, could out-run any short-legged, shaggy-hided Indian pony on the plains.

The young rider circled to see what it was the coyotes and buzzards had been working over. There had been other such scavengers a few miles back but he believed them to be interested in a buffalo carcass, thousands of which were left on the plains by careless hunters.

When he came up close now, though, he sat his saddle stock-still, staring down at what was left of a scalped corpse.

"Lewis Miller!" he gasped.

12

He tried to raise his eyes and look at the other object nearby. That took a terrific mental effort, for he knew what he might find. He gritted his teeth, and looked. And even from where he sat Bucky he recognized familiar clothing. His father's! All thought of any possible danger to himself left him as he fought against sudden, overwhelming grief.

Dismounting, he knelt beside what was left of the corpse of his father. The mark of the Sioux was upon Barringer Senior, and near the body were three eagle feathers, dyed with berry juices, such as the savages used in their bonnets and hair.

The shock hit young Jim Barringer hard. He bit his lip until the blood ran, striving to control his grief and trembling, his flesh crawling with horror.

But one thing had been instilled in him through all his young life. Men on the Frontier matured young, and even boys knew that they must face death like men.

From the dark-shadowed spot marking the drywash cut, the tip of an eagle feather showed over the grass top, ruffled by the breeze, but although young Jim's keen eyes subconsciously saw it, he was too stunned now to take alarm and flee.

But there was no swooping attack from the cut.

He took his long-bladed hunting knife and began to dig up the sod, six feet of it, working feverishly, swiftly — anything to dull his sharp grief. His hard knuckles struck sharp stones and bled as he made a shallow grave for his father's remains. Laying his father in the hole he dug, and shoveling back the dirt, he gathered more rocks to keep the coyotes out.

"I'll come back and do a good job later, Dad," he muttered. "But — how'll I tell Ma and Sis?"

Still there was no movement at the ravine. As he regained his self-control somewhat, his trained eyes began noting signs in the surrounding earth, the print of a shod hoof, and then a cork, which still smelled of whiskey. Searching further, on his hands and knees, he located a number of boot marks, one of which was oversized, with its heel definitely marked by an "X" — a cross of nails "to keep the devil away."

Nothing yet from the ravine.

Bucky nosed his master's arm uneasily, then a new sound caused Jim Barringer to look up quickly, across the shimmering plains. The sound was the creaking of a large wooden wagon wheel on a bulky iron axle that needed grease.

And he could see the billowing top of a prairie schooner heading his way.

That brought him out of his preoccupation of grief. He glanced quickly at the ravine where he was sure murderous Sioux were lurking, and sprang to his saddle, riding full-tilt toward the wagon train. It was not a large one, being composed of only half a dozen big wagons.

On the driver's seat of the leading wagon, with the reins of the plodding truck horses in her hands, sat a girl whose reddish-gold hair was stirred by the breeze, a girl with the loveliness of budding maturity. She wore a gray dress, and her sunbonnet lay on the seat beside her. There was a merry gleam in her deep blue eyes.

As young Jim Barringer raised his arm, signaling the procession, she turned a laughing face, pretty as a picture, to him as he reined Bucky to a dusty stop.

"And what's your hurry, sir?" she called. "You nearly made old Whitey balk!"

"Where's yore wagon boss, ma'am?" Barringer asked soberly, glancing back over his shoulder.

"Who are you, and what's your name?" she demanded.

"No time for that now, ma'am." Jim said quickly. A burly man in a brown shirt and trousers, his burnished hair giving off a copper gleam, jumped from the back of the wagon and came toward him. "Pull yore wagons around into a circle, fast, mister," Barringer commanded. "There's Sioux over in that ravine!"

"Ye don't say, young feller!" exclaimed the burly man, his chin dropping.

"Pronto — hurry," insisted Jim, dismounting to help. "I don't know how many there are, but they're waitin' for yuh."

He understood now why he had not been attacked. The Indians in the cut had not wanted to alarm the approaching train.

A woman's sharp cry came from the front wagon, and Jim Barringer saw that the red-haired girl was staring with wide-open eyes at the drywash. From it, as from a magical opening in the earth, Indians were pouring, mounted on fleet little shaggy-hided mustangs with tails and manes braided with ribbons.

They were Sioux, as Barringer had guessed, big copper-skinned braves in leather pants or breech clouts.

15

They were painted with savage beauty for war, with stripes on their cheeks, and armed to the teeth with the finest firearms Government money could buy.

When they realized they had been discovered they set up an unearthly whooping, bearing down straight at the emigrant train.

"Come down here!" Jim ordered.

Seizing the frightened girl in his powerful arms he lifted her to the ground and ran with her around behind the heavy wooden body of the wagon. He placed her inside the schooner.

"Mind yuh keep yore head down, now!" he commanded her.

Bullets and feathered arrows hailed on them. A tall man who stood, frozen and gaping, suddenly clapped his hand to his side and knotted over, bitten by a slug.

Coolly Jim Barringer seized the reins of the lead wagon and yanked the big horses around. The other drivers followed, forming a rough enclosure. For, aside from the buffalo wallows, there was no cover from which to fight.

Jim had Bucky behind a schooner, protecting his mount. He seized his Sharps and took aim at a Sioux sub-chief who had ridden in dangerously close.

The buffalo gun roared. The sub-chief threw up both hands and crashed dead. Two Indians yanked their ponies to a dead stop on the instant and picked him up. Jim Barringer, well knowing this Indian custom of saving wounded and dead so the enemy could not count coup on them, wounded one of the rescuers.

"Get yore guns goin'!" he roared at the emigrant men.

A scattering fire opened up from behind the ring of wagons. Women began to scream as their white faces peered out anxiously.

"Greenhorns, pilgrims, everyone of 'em," thought Barringer.

It was with dismay, not so much at his own fate as because of what would happen to them that he saw Sioux keep on pouring from the ravine. Thick and fast they came, until he knew there must be more than two hundred. He could have outridden them on Buck — but that was not the way of the plainsman.

CHAPTER
THREE

Meat for the Road

Bob Pryor, handsome, lithe, known throughout the Frontier as the Rio Kid, yawned as he shot his last buffalo to make up the day's quota. Each hunter for the hungry hordes working on the railroad had to supply twelve head of the great beasts every morning, and Pryor added an extra carcass to make up a baker's dozen for good measure. Goddard Brothers, who contracted to feed the Union Pacific laborers, hired only expert buffalo hunters.

His .50 caliber rifle was growing hot in the octagonal barrel and it was time to cool it off. He stopped his mouse-colored dun, Saber, his horse that was known almost as well as its rider, and began attending to his weapon as a trained soldier or plainsman should.

Another heavy gun roared not far away and he watched his crony and partner, Buffalo Bill Cody, on Brigham, a wise and expert creature at hunting on the plains, down a shaggy-maned bull. Brigham, a mount trained by Cody himself knew every move that must be made, putting his rider in perfect position and allowing a second shot in case the first missed.

"That mustang is most as smart as you, Saber," Pryor teased his own horse, and the dun sniffed at his hand; as if he understood.

Not long ago the Rio Kid had been Captain Robert Pryor of the Union Cavalry, riding under General George A. Custer in Sheridan's divisions. Born on the Rio Grande, from which his nickname came, he had fought through four terrible years of brotherly strife, the worst sort of warfare.

The horrors seen on the battlefield had left some mark upon him, but his blue eyes had not lost their youthful light, their devil-may-care recklessness. His smooth bronzed cheeks glowed with the health of a man who lives always out-of-doors, busy at hard physical tasks. Broad at the shoulders, the Rio Kid tapered off to the narrow waist of the ace fighting man. A cavalry Stetson covered his warm chestnut hair. Once he had liked his hair cropped short, for he had a passion for neatness, inborn, and developed to a fetich in his Army life.

However, he had not needed the advice of Buffalo Bill and others, when he had come into the Sioux country, to realize that he must flaunt a lengthy scalp to maintain the respect of the savages. They had no use for a man who dared not wear his hair long. So he had allowed it to grow somewhat, although it did not touch his shoulders as did Cody's.

Mustered out at the end of the War, he was still a soldier at heart, although he had now gained a reputation as a scout, second to none. His soldierly feeling was expressed in his clothing for usually he wore, as now, blue breeches, with a faded yellow stripe down the seams, tucked into expensive shiny boots with Army spurs. His blue shirt, the V at the neck disclosing his powerful chest, suggested the soldier. At his lean waist was a three-inch-wide black sword belt, and cartridge belts carried ammunition for his two visible Colt .45s. Always following the method of a smart officer, however, two more revolvers rode in shoulder holsters out of sight.

Four years as a cavalryman had made him a deadly shot from horseback, and Saber, the dun with the black stripe down his backbone, "the breed that never dies," was trained to a T. Throughout the Rio Kid's martial career, Saber had been his mount, and the fiery dun thrived on the smoke of battle.

Yet though a war veteran, this great scout was, in years, hardly more than a youth. War had matured but had not killed his sense of humor and zest for life either. Rather it had made him restless and eager for excitement. A humdrum existence would never do for the Rio Kid.

It needed but a single glance to see that this man was a leader. Just as any man who was a judge of horseflesh would at once have sized up the horse the Rio Kid rode.

Saber was bony and log of leg. He did not look like a racer, but he could run like a streak and in battle was an equine devil. At the bang of guns he had to be restrained from running in to share in the fighting. He was hardly sweet-tempered, save with his master, and was given to lashing out and bullying other mustangs.

20

When angry, his eyes would roll in his flattened-eared head, one orb mirled with blue and white streaks through the brown iris.

Handsome as a bronzed young god was the Rio Kid, with his clean-cut features and deep blue eyes. And not only his looks, but his bravery attracted the fair sex. For his own part, a beautiful girl charmed and fascinated him, but realizing that he was a rolling stone who would never be happy to settle down, he was aware he was no bargain. The War had done that to him, as it had to many thousands of other young fellows. Good reason why, on the Frontier, from Mexico to Canada, good men for a scrap could always be found . . .

"Lucretia Borgia," as Buffalo Bill called his needle gun, spouted smoke and lead once more. Then Cody, the young scout and hunter who was already famous throughout the West, turned Brigham, his own mount, and trotted over to his friend, the Rio Kid,

Cody dismounted, dropping his reins, taking care that Brigham was not within kicking or biting distance of the saturnine Saber.

He quickly wiped the dust, caked by perspiration, from his broad high forehead.

He was about the Rio Kid's height, just under six feet. He had beautiful flowing brown hair reaching to his broad shoulders, a mustache and small goatee of the same hue, and his large brown eyes were friendly and frank. His complexion, although tanned by sun and wind, was definitely fair. He wore fringed buckskin and moccasins, and a felt hat with a wide brim — the comfortable and efficient costume of the plainsman.

"I'm starved, Bob," he said, squatting beside Pryor. "Reckon we can take our ride up the Loup Fork like we planned? We're through early."

"Yeah, but we had to ride out farther, Bill. I tell yuh, the buffalo are gettin' scarcer."

Cody shrugged. "It'll take a long time to finish off the millions on the plains, Kid. The sooner the better, so General Sheridan figgers. Then the Sioux won't be able to scalp our folks. They live on the buffalo."

The two scouts ate a cold meal in companionable silence. It did not take them long to dispose of the jerked meat, the hard bread and flask of warm water. Buffalo Bill passed the "makin's" to the Rio Kid who rolled one and was about to light up when Cody remarked:

"That's our wagon, I reckon. Butcher's sort of slow catchin' up —"

"Like the devil!" exploded Pryor, who was in a better position to see than was his friend. "Get mounted, fast, Bill!"

The wind was from the west, so that the approaching dust that had been the first thing to attract the Rio Kid's keen attention had not been carried even to the keener nostrils of the beasts as warning. Expecting his trail comrade, Celestino Mireles, the lean Mexican boy, who was his protege, to be coming up with the butcher wagons which would carry the beef back to Junction City, Bob Pryor had not been as alert as usual, nor had Buffalo Bill. They were not more than twelve miles from the graders out ahead of the tracks, and things had been quiet for the past few days.

22

And now, as they leaped to saddle, speeding away, they were cut off from the grading camp by an intervening band of red riders that had stolen up on them! They rode in the only direction they could, forced westward along the Platte, glimmering in the distance.

"Are they Sioux — yeah, they are," called Cody, after he had taken a look over his buckskin-clad shoulder.

He was loading Lucretia Borgia, guiding Brigham with his knees, while the Rio Kid was already prepared for a long shot.

"Range is mighty long," Pryor called back. "Fifty of 'em comin', Bill! I hope they didn't get the butcher wagons!"

"Durn 'em, they'll ruin our day's kill!" growled Cody. "We'll hafta work overtime, Bob, to make up for it."

The two dozen buffalo they had shot were lying in a fairly small area, to make it easier for the butchers.

"Brule Sioux — some of Spotted Tail's gang!" the Rio Kid yelled at Cody, as he fired.

A hairy Indian mustang fell, the rider landing on his feet, running. He leaped up behind one of his mates with hardly a break in pace. The Sioux began to whoop, now that they could not surprise the two whites.

They were broad, burly savages, streaked in the face, and with eagle feathers in their black scalp locks. Many were naked save for breechcloths. Implacable, sworn to fight the white man to the death in defense of the buffalo range, the Sioux was a tough customer. War had been declared by Sitting Bull, Gall and other chiefs.

And their allies, the Cheyennes and Kiowas, were fighting along with them.

"Spotted Tail done sent word that the tracks wasn't to go no farther," grunted Cody, "and I reckon he meant it."

There were too many for the pair to smash alone, with no cover from which to fight. The Sioux were brave and would rush them. It was simply a question of outrunning them, then circling around to reach Junction City.

The two fleeing men did not shoot back often, since that would be a waste of ammunition at such range. On and on they raced, keeping low over their mounts, with the Indians gradually falling behind the long-legged Saber and Brigham. Both scouts had been forced to out-run such hostile bands before.

The plains kept holding out mirages, as if waves of a land ocean were higher just ahead. However, when the next summit was breasted, it would be found that the crest ahead was only slightly higher, and when that was reached, the same thing occurred. This deceived men not used to the plains, but both Cody and Pryor were well acquainted with this phenomenon.

"Still comin', the red fools," muttered Buffalo Bill as they slowed to breathe their horses after a two hours' run. Later and dust coated the heaving animals. "They must savvy they'll never catch up with us."

The Sioux were specks in the distance, but still coming.

"Well, mebbe they're hopin' one of our hosses'll step in a gopher hole —" the Rio Kid had begun, but he broke off, straining his ears. Cody heard the same thing from up ahead.

"Gunfire!" he exclaimed. "And real heavy!"

The Rio Kid nodded, and trotted Saber on.

"I s'pose that gang back there figgered we'd run into their pards up here. Let's have a look-see."

They breasted several of the prairie sea's static waves, before they saw anything. But the shooting was heavy, as Cody had said. Then a madly riding ring of Sioux that Bob Pryor hastily estimated at near two hundred, interposed between them and half a dozen wagons drawn into a rough barricade.

The draught horses that had been hitched to the prairie schooners had all been killed. Some had died from Indian bullets, while others, maddened by fear and threatening to run away, had been dispatched by the whites inside the wagon barricade.

Rifles and pistols banged from the wagons. The Indians were circling, one of their favorite maneuvers. Evidently they had grown tired of direct charges, which had cost them dearly in life and horseflesh.

"By all that's hot," exclaimed the Rio Kid, throwing his rifle to his shoulders, "there's Spotted Tail hisself, Bill!"

A magnificent Sioux, in a full headdress of eagle feathers with tips dyed red, yellow and blue, his face streaked with war markings, bronzed body naked save for a doeskin belt and two cartridge slings over his broad shoulders, led the attack. He was a magnificent savage figure on a pink-and-white warhorse, its tail and mane braided with ribbons.

But before the Rio Kid could draw a proper bead, Sioux watchers on the nearby crests set up a whooping and started for the two scouts. Spotted Tail, head chief of the Brule Sioux, jerked his rope halter and his handsome mustang swerved just as Pryor fired.

Always wary and watchful for a surprise, at which they themselves so delighted, the Indians shifted their attention from the wagons and started for Cody and Pryor.

CHAPTER
FOUR

Pawnees to the Rescue

Working fast, Buffalo Bill's guns were echoing the Rio Kid's. Neither wasted any lead. But there were too many Sioux to stand against in the open, and although the Indians were notoriously poor shots with a rifle, their volleys were dangerously close.

Reluctantly the two scouts swung their horses and retreated, riding away from both Spotted Tail's band and the approaching Sioux gang which had previously been pursuing them.

The Indians who had been after the emigrants caught the metal-flashed signals of their oncoming friends. It told them they had nothing to fear, outside of these two lone whites.

"They been here for awhile, and that's luck for us," observed the Rio Kid, as he and his companion stubbornly retreated, contesting the way with the Sioux. "Their hosses are as wore out as ours."

Many Indians who had been after the wagons had drawn off to chase the scouts. But Spotted Tail waved and shouted commands, and the main forces returned to the chief objective, leaving a small group to fend off the Rio Kid and his partner, Buffalo Bill.

"We got to fetch help for them wagon folks, Bill," declared Pryor. "They look like greenhorns, though they got theirselves in a good position, seein' as they were surprised. But most of 'em don't shoot good."

"There's one who does!" exclaimed Cody, as a rifle barked from the wagons and an Indian sub-chief fell off his horse. "That was a Sharps, Bob."

"You reckon we can reach the Pawnee village on the Loup Fork?"

"I guess we got to!"

They started riding swiftly again. But they had only run a few miles from the besieged wagon train when Cody jerked his reins, pointing off to the right.

"Look at that, Rio Kid!"

"Whoopee!" shouted the man on the dun.

He gave the shrill yell learned from the Rebels in the war, that high-pitched, blood-curdling, fighting challenge, a mixture of hate, derision and triumph which carried for miles on the wind.

Waving their Stetsons, the two buffalo hunters rode to meet the oncoming band they had seen — some threescore men with a tall, rangy leader. He raised a thin arm to stop his followers, facing the two who slid to a stop, sweated and dusty.

"Hey, Major!" shouted the Rio Kid. "We was comin' after yuh! The Sioux are out thick as hide bugs on a dead buffalo!"

"Howdy, Frank," Buffalo Bill greeted, grinning.

Both scouts were well acquainted with Major Frank North, the white Chief of the Pawnees. A few years older than Cody and the Rio Kid, his reputation on the Frontier was tremendous.

He wore a regular Army officer's uniform, with a major's insignia. His slouch hat shaded deep-set, straight-looking eyes. He had a high, intelligent forehead, his face narrowing to a sharp chin, and a short black mustache was over his wide, friendly mouth. Bold and brave as a lion, diffident and unassuming, he was a natural leader. The hero of a hundred hair-raising clashes, Frank North had become a legendary figure in the land.

"Yes," he replied quietly, "I've been huntin' for those Sioux, boys. They burned a station last night near Cottonwood Springs. Which way?"

"We'll show yuh," the Rio Kid said. "It ain't far, Major."

North raised his hand. "Follow me, men," he ordered. "Lieutenant Murie, make sure everything's in order for a fight."

"Follow me." Frank North never said, "Go ahead," but "Come on," to his men.

The dark-faced Indians enlisted under him as regular Army scouts were Pawnees, friendly to the whites and the deadly enemies of the Sioux, who had descimated their tribes in wars throughout the centuries. From the Pawnee reservation on the Loup Fork of the Platte, Major Frank North had recruited his strange but extremely efficient and valuable battalion.

They were big men, many standing inches over six feet and weighing two hundred and twenty or thirty pounds. Each Pawnee, supplied with a regular cavalry uniform, had retained of it what he considered important. Some, despite the hot sun, wore heavy overcoats, but no trousers, wearing breechclout instead. In many instances feet were bare, and brass spurs were tied about ankles.

Others wore regulation pants but no shirt, while yet others had cut out the entire seat of their trousers. Many had kept the large black Army hat, wearing it strapped on a dark head. But enough were bare-headed to show the traditional Pawnee haircut, with the skull shaved bare on both sides of a high-standing narrow strip which stood up a couple of inches and looked like a horn.

The Pawnees had rendered valuable service to the Army, acting as advance scouts, always being the first to locate hostile Indians. Now they were helping guard the track-layers.

Brave and very able fighting men, everybody liked them and admired them.

At first, officers had attempted to make regular soldiers of them, but this had proved impossible. Finally, they had left the Pawnees to Major North, whom the Indians loved and would follow to the death.

Armed with Spencer carbines, seven-shooters, long scalping-knives and revolvers, and with a loyalty to Major North above that given even their own chiefs, the Pawnees rode after North, Cody and the Rio Kid.

It did not take long to make the run. The Sioux who had been after Cody and Bob Pryor saw them coming and turned to flee.

"Spotted Tail's down below with a couple hundred after that wagon train, Major," Pryor reported.

North nodded. "Lieutenant Murie!" he called.

An officer rode up, saluted.

"Take fifteen men and bear down on the right flank as we go in."

In the Pawnee tongue he spoke to a huge Indian who weighed nearly two hundred and fifty pounds and stood six-feet-four in his bare feet. "Big Spotted Horse," he ordered, "you go with Murie."

Big Spotted Horse saluted.

"Yes, Pawnee La Shar."

North was their beloved chief, Pawnee Chief, "Grandfather." They had called him "Father" when he had been a captain.

Now he was a major, and had to be promoted accordingly in Pawnee language.

The Pawnees were livening up for the battle. Tomahawks were touched, to make sure they were in place; cartridges for the Spencer carbines made ready.

Smoke was in the sky from the burning wagon, fired by flaming arrows. Dust rose, guns roared, but began dying off as the Pawnees drove in, led by Major North, Cody, and the Rio Kid. For the Sioux would not stand against the Pawnees.

Trained at tactics and in orderly formation, the Pawnees lined out at the bugle's clear commands. Saber snorted and pranced over, trying to take his place as a cavalry captain's horse should. His mirled eye rolled, and he lifted his forelegs proudly.

Down past the deep ravine guttered the Sioux, as the Spencers barked, their whiplike voices sharp on the west wind. Savages who had been left lying on the plain at the hasty withdrawal were dispatched by Pawnee knives and tomahawks, the Indian soldiers leaping off, killing and scalping with hardly a pause.

With Spotted Tail and his nefarious braves on their way, the Rio Kid left the pursuit to the efficient Major North and his men. Because Saber was run out and he himself was saddle-stiff and thirsty, he swung back to the canvas-topped schooners.

He sang out, raising his hand in greeting. Hoarse-voiced men cheered, and a girl appeared suddenly from behind a bullet-marked wagon. The west wind blew the red-gold hair abut her pretty oval face, pale now and serious. She wore a wide-skirted gray dress and, the Rio Kid decided, she was not yet twenty. Her deep blue eyes sought his frankly.

"Good afternoon, ma'am," drawled the Rio Kid. She seemed so shocked and frightened that he sought to lighten her with a jest. "I see yuh're a newcomer to these parts. After this, never stop and speak to an Indian unless yuh have an Army with yuh."

Her gaze widened, then she smiled, a merry light making her eyes like twin diamonds. A dimple showed in her peach-bloom cheek and when she answered him he knew she was Irish.

"We were so glad to see you coming that I nearly cried," she told him. "Then you rode away and we were so disappointed I almost cried. And when you came up just now — well. I'm nearly crying!"

"The Sioux are out mighty thick today," the Rio Kid said. "Yore train's purty small to be this far out with no escort. It's the kind of outfit they're huntin' for — not too big, but enough for loot and prisoners."

"My father's leader of the train, sir," the girl said proudly. "We were so eager to find our new land, we started right along."

A couple of dead men were sprawled out inside the small circle, as well as the carcasses of the big horses, and bullets had slashed the wooden sides of the wagons. Feathered arrows stuck thick in the outer defenses. Smoke, acrid and penetrating, puffed up from the smoldering schooner, while men with bleeding wounds waited for help.

The women, mothers and daughters, and the children, were coming out from their hiding places in the big carts, to do their part. Water was being broken out, and congratulations were in order.

Two men stepped from between the leading wagons.

"Good, sir," cried the burly one with the broad, genial face, reddened and pleated by the sun, "we've a lot to thank ye for! Bless you for snatchin' us from those red imps of Satan!" He seized Pryor's hand and pumped it.

"This is my father," said the girl. "Michael McClean. I'm Elsa. We're from County Cork, the most of us."

"Never mind thankin' me," the Rio Kid said quickly. "Wait till Major North and his Pawnees get back, ma'am. They call me the Rio Kid — Bob Pryor on paper. We happened to be buffalo huntin' and a bunch of the Sioux run us over this way."

A tall, stalwart young man with a frown on his handsome face spoke up.

"So you're the Rio Kid. I know yuh."

Bob Pryor turned on him. "I've seen yuh somewhere, haven't I?"

"Yeah. I'm Jim Barringer. Live near Riverside — the Slantin' B Ranch. I saw yuh at the railroad camp one day with Buffalo Bill."

Elsa McClean turned her wonderful smile on young Barringer.

"This young man has been a fine help to us," she said quickly. "He warned us of the savages and fought for us — though he was too busy to tell his name before!"

Barringer flushed as McClean slapped him on the back.

"He showed us how to hold 'em off," the girl's father declared. "He was dropped like an angel from on high to save us."

Men and women crowded around to greet the Rio Kid. Most of them were emigrants from Ireland, lured by the glowing prospectuses of the railroad companies to the farming lands of Nebraska and the new country the steel lines opened up. From every nation in the world traveling agents were sending settlers, some with money, others poor and forlorn, hoping for a start in the promised land of the United States.

The fertility, the mineral wealth, the balmy summers and good water were all stressed by expert writers, but nothing was ever said about the heart-breaking toil necessary in starting a farm and ranch, nothing pictured about the difficulties of transportation, and never a word about the red killers lying in wait. And the fact that in the central and northern states the winters were as murderous as any Indian, that the plains offered no timber for building and fuel, so that the pioneers must live in hastily constructed sod-houses, was somehow ignored by these splendid descriptive word-painters.

The Irish accent and the talk amused the Rio Kid, and the frank friendliness of Elsa McClean would have animated a wooden Indian, although her smile was for Jim Barringer as well as Bob Bryor.

Pryor pitched in, as did Jim Barringer, at helping clean up the camp. Graves were dug, and the stones saved to make protective cairns over the mounds. Men dragged the wagons off from the bloody ground, and built fires of buffalo chips as Barringer and Pryor taught them to. An evening meal was set a-cooking.

The Rio Kid's keen gaze did not miss young Jim Barringer's tortured eyes when Jim thought no one was watching. And he noted how the youth worked feverishly, and did not even smile when Elsa McClean beamed upon him.

"Somethin' hit him hard," mused Pryor.

CHAPTER
FIVE

Land of Promise

The time flew on wings, and soon dark was upon them. Pryor put sentries out to watch for any return of hostiles, and squatted around the smoldering fire of buffalo chips, digging into the bowl of stew Elsa brought him.

Barringer was back in the shadows. He ate, but listlessly. The Rio Kid edged over toward him.

"Jim," he said, his voice low and lost in the animated talk of the excited emigrants, "what's eatin' on yuh? Somethin' hit yuh hard. Can I help?"

Barringer turned his tortured eyes upon Bob Pryor. He did not answer for a time, and seemed about to draw into himself. Then he caught the kind gleam in Pryor's eyes.

"My father was kilt, not far from here," he muttered. "Murdered, scalped, and robbed — him and two friends."

He described how he had found the remains.

"The Sioux?" asked the Rio Kid.

Barringer shook his head. "I think white men done it, mister."

The Rio Kid was startled.

"Who?" he demanded.

"I dunno," the young plainsman said grimly, "but I mean to find out. Whoever it was had outsize feet and a cross in the heel of his boot to keep the devil away. Look — I found these close to Dad's corpse." He held out several empty cartridge shells to Pryor. "He was riddled with bullets."

Pryor, expert about firearms, examined the shell cases closely.

"Forty-five caliber Colt six-shooter, a bit off center," he murmured. "Funny scratches the hammer makes. Looks like Bigboots stood over yore dad and emptied his gun into him just from hate. Then he ejected the shells and reloaded. Lemme keep one of these, Jim. Yuh could shore pin it on the man if yuh ever could locate that gun. It leaves a trademark."

"There's an awful lot of Colt forty-fives out here, though."

A guard at the lower end of camp called a warning and Pryor jumped up, seizing his carbine. But it was Major North, Buffalo Bill and the Pawnee scouts coming in. They rode up, dusty, lathered and tired. The Sioux, according to their custom, had split up into a hundred small units and taken every which direction, to meet later at some prearranged destination. Many had escaped but the big Pawnees looked satisfied, and dripping scalps hung from many belts.

McClean and the emigrants were shaking hands with the tall, lean North, giving their heart-felt thanks. But gratitude and attention embarrassed the diffident North.

"I only did what I'm paid for," he said. "In fact, I was lookin' for Spotted Tail when I got the alarm."

Food was handed out to the red scouts. The Pawnees were good-natured and friendly. They circulated through the camp, looking over what interested them and speaking now and then a word of English they had learned.

The emigrants were nervous, so near the tall, strangly-clad savages. The fierce, high-boned faces, hawk beaks, beady black eyes, the bloody tomahawks and the gory scalps were not reassuring.

Elsa's red hair caught the firelight, threw it back with the scintillations of shiny red copper. A huge scout in fringed legging-moccasins, his torso naked and big around as a barrel, and with four Sioux scalps hanging from his doeskin belt, reached out his great hand and caught her long tresses.

"Let go, you — you red fiend!" Elsa cried out.

She slapped the Pawnee who, looking injured, dropped her braid. The Rio Kid smiled. Major North spoke softly in the Pawnee tongue. The brave grinned and backed off.

"He didn't mean any harm, ma'am," North assured. "That's Traveling Bear, one of my best scouts. He was only admiring your hair. He hasn't often seen red hair and he says yours is the finest yet."

"Well, so long as he doesn't add it to his collection," Elsa said, managing to smile again. "If my heart ever beats normally again, I'll be surprised!"

Major North put several of his scouts out around the emigrant camp.

38

"I'll see you to yore destination, McClean," he said. "Since the Sioux are out in force, I can't let you travel without an escort."

They were worn out from their ordeal. Women and children went to bed in the big wagons, while the men rolled in blankets underneath or around the smoky fires.

Suddenly, from down the line, a Pawnee sentry shrieked:

"Pass three dollars, half-past go to hell!"

Major North grinned at the Rio Kid.

"That's as close as Sky Chief ever gets to 'Post Number Three, half-past nine, all is well.'"

Before the sun reddened the sky, the camp was roused. North had captured a number of Indian mustangs and the more tractable of the Army horses were hitched to the prairie schooners.

"How 'bout it, Bob?" asked Buffalo Bill. "Shall we head back to Junction City or go on a ways with these folks?"

"I vote we give 'em a start, anyways, Bill."

The little train made ready to start west after a quick breakfast. As Bob Pryor was swallowing some scalding coffee from a tin cup, he turned at a loud hail. A young Mexican in a wide sombrero and a dark velvet suit came tearing up to him, threw himself from his horse beside the Rio Kid.

"General! You are here! I theenk ze Sioux hav' keel you!"

"Howdy, Celestino. So yuh trailed us."

"*Si*, General. Ees aw-ful. Ze butchair, he turn hees wag-on back and say 'I got en-gagement, I forget.' I come on as fast as I can."

The dark face of Celestino Mireles, the Rio Kid's trail-mate and constant friend, had a proud cast. The high-bridged nose was curved like an eagle's beak. His eyes and hair were jet-black. Into his wide red sash, his pistols and the long knife he favored at close quarters were thrust.

Hidalgo blood from old Castile flowed in Celestino's veins. The Rio Kid had snatched him from death, across the Rio Grande when the lad's father and people had been slain by criminals who were later disposed of by Bob Pryor. Celestino had followed the Rio Kid ever since, offering a doglike devotion.

After greeting his trail-mate, the Rio Kid got up on the wagon box beside Elsa McClean. These horses were not easily handled, for they were not broken to draught work. He had to manage four of them, each of which believed in having its own way.

Saber trotted out in position with the column of scouts, as if he were back in the Army. Jim Barringer, on a mustang borrowed from Major North, had another dead friend to add to his list. Bucky, his horse, had been slain in the Sioux attack.

Elsa McClean's blue eyes strained westward for a view of the promised home in this fresh virgin country.

"It's mighty flat, isn't it?" she remarked after a time to the Rio Kid, who was concentrating on keeping the four skittish animals from running away, tangling into a knot or fighting. "I keep thinking there'll be something

40

interesting over the next rise but it's always the same. Just another crest ahead."

He smiled, the sun wrinkles at the corners of his handsome eyes deepening. He knew these flats and their monotony. The buffalo loved them and so did the Sioux, dashing madly over them in pursuit of food and enemies, but they were appallingly wearisome to a civilized woman or man used to broken country of trees and rocks and lakes.

Ever on and on ran the great plains, always to be known as the "Great American Desert." Its vastness dwarfed everything else. The curling grass rustled under the iron-bound wheels and in the distance the wide, shallow Platte went its calm way, while buffalo grazed stolidly.

At noon the wagon train paused for half an hour. Michael McClean, buoyant and confident, was also a natural leader. Elsa's mother had died the year before, one of his reasons for emigrating. He was a farmer and loved the soil. The dirt he ran through his stubby, calloused fingers seemed to please him.

"It's foine earth, though it needs trees," he observed.

"It'll grow anything, Mister," Barringer told him.

"That's a fact," the Rio Kid said with a solemn face. "Leave yore rifle stock in the ground at night and in the mornin' yuh'll pick bullets."

The emigrants roared with laughter. They loved to jest.

"How far you want to go?" Major North inquired.

"Well, now," replied McClean, "in Omaha they told us we'd find free land about here."

41

"It's a long way off from anywheres," observed Jim Barringer. "Why don't yuh settle near Riverside, McClean? There's still some good sections yuh can take up there. The water's better'n usual and some mighty fine folks live around. Besides, winter's comin' on and yuh won't have time to settle as yuh should. Our folks would be glad to give yuh a hand, show yuh how to build a soddy and so on."

"That's mighty kind of ye, young man," McClean replied earnestly. "We'll consider it, and we thank ye."

This trip was becoming much to the Rio Kid's liking, for buffalo hunting was beginning to pall on him. Though the pay was high and he had plenty of money in his belt, he welcomed the excuse to break the monotonous grind. One buffalo was just like another, and none offered any excitement. He and Cody were under contract to deliver twelve buffalo each per day but were ahead of the game and could afford to lay off awhile.

However, on the following morning Buffalo Bill decided to start back. Pryor sent Celestino with Cody, telling the Mexican to attend to his share of the hunting until he should return to Junction City. Mireles could hire a skinner and do as well as Pryor.

The Rio Kid was much interested in the wagon train — and in Elsa McClean, whose ebullient spirits gave him a lift. Not only was she pretty, but with her happy, excitable nature she could never be down-hearted for long and was always ready to laugh at Bob Pryor's jests.

CHAPTER
SIX

Where Will the Railroad Go

A day later the wagon train arrived at Riverside. the Nebraska settlement on the Wood River, the place young Jim Barringer called home. Bluffs rose on the banks, and a belt of timber grew along both sides of the stream, which eventually emptied into the Platte. The growth was scrubby, for wood was scarce and the early settlers had cut off the larger trees.

There were only three dirt streets in the town, with a community pump in a central square, which was bare of grass. Most of the buildings were of sod, made of great chunks of the plains soil cut into bricks, although a few more imposing structures were of logs and raw boards, or sheet-iron, every square foot of it freighted in by mule and ox train. Farms and ranches stretched away in the distance.

When the wagon creaked up into the plaza, the Rio Kid turned and grinned at Elsa.

"Oh, dear!" she exclaimed, making a wry face. "Is — is this it? From what Jim said, I thought it would be like Dublin!"

Bob Pryor laughed. "These plains towns are all alike, Elsa. Mud when it's wet, dust when it's dry, and flatter'n warm rain-water! Now if yuh want to see somethin', try Texas or the Rockies!"

"It's not a bad place," Jim Barringer growled.

Two tears trickled from the girl's deep-blue eyes, and rolled down her pink cheeks. She was looking now at the promised land and it did not come up to anticipation. But her father was again on his knees, testing the earth. He was smiling.

Not until the Rio Kid leaped down and reached up to set Elsa on the ground did he realize how his arms ached from the pull on the reins. The broncs had calmed down after their first wild display, but they still did not know how to draw a wagon.

He was surprised to see how lively the settlement was. Wagons piled with furniture and household goods stood in front of many homes, while a crowd was collected in the plaza, listening to a fat man who stood on a flat-topped cart speaking to them.

"Movin' day," the Rio Kid remarked. "What goes on, Jim?"

Barringer shrugged. "Yuh got me, Kid. I'll go see."

McClean's people crowded around the town pump, happy to have plenty of water at last. Elsa was trying to hide her disappointment as the Rio Kid squeezed her hand and left with Barringer for the gathering of townspeople who piad little attention to the wagon train. Such sights were common enough, and they were preoccupied.

"I tell yuh, folks," the stout man on the wagon was yelling, "I seen the surveyors layin' out the line down there! They even made a cut where the bridge'll be!"

The flaccid speaker with the popping, pale blue eyes was in a dither of excitement. He wore a tattered blue shirt, blue overalls covered with dust, and cow boots. His stringy brown hair was flapping in the breeze.

"What's got Chickenhead Sims so excited, Warren?" Barringer asked a heavy-set, solemn-faced man on the outskirts of the crowd. "Where's everybody goin' to? Looks like the whole town's movin'."

"Sims seen railroad surveyors layin' out the line thirty mile south of here," the heavy-set man replied. "They say the U.P.'s goin' to cross the river there at Dogtooth Gap and not here at all. Folks figer on settlin' down there."

"Leave their homes?" cried Barringer.

"Well, yuh know how it is. There's a fortune in bein' close to where the railroad'll run. Did yuh locate yore dad, Jim?"

"I found him, Warren," Jim Barringer said, his youthful jaw grim and hard. "Scalped, murdered! And Miller and Ulman along with him."

The other man groaned.

He put a kind and sympathetic hand on the youth's broad and manly shoulder.

"I'm mighty sorry, boy. It's a hard world, a bitter world. Can I do anything to help yuh?"

"Reckon there ain't nothin' to do now . . . This is Bob Pryor, Warren, called the Rio Kid. Bob, meet Warren Grebe. He owns the hotel here."

"Glad to know yuh, Grebe," said the Rio Kid, shaking hands. He had already taken the man in from his brown eyes and wide nose to his brown suit and heavy boots and the big ears that stuck from beneath his neat, straight brown hat. "So that fat hombre claims he knows where the railroad will run, does he?"

"I'm pullin' out at dawn, folks!" "Chickenhead" Sims was yelling in a high-pitched voice. "Take my advice and come along. The railroad folks tried to fool us by sayin' they might come through here but it ain't so. They want to hog all the best land, even if they have to settle dummies around to get control. There's millions in it, millions! And at Dogtooth Gap is shore where the U.P.'s goin' through!"

The fever of Sims' words had fired the town. Though it was familiar enough, this land-grabbing excitement. Everybody wanted to be on the new line, which would swell land values, bringing enormous profits for those in the right spots. Whole towns would move overnight on a tip.

The Rio Kid had bumped into this before, as the U.P. had slowly pushed westward. There was great speculation in land and town sites ahead of the rails. While the road owned so many sections and had right of eminent domain on its way, there was plenty of opportunity for big fortunes to be made by speculators. Car shops at a certain settlement would mean the place would be a center of industry, lots worth hundreds of dollars each.

McClean and his friends, having washed up, were strolling over to join the crowd. Over on a shaded porch, the Rio Kid saw a man he knew, a crooked gambler known along the line as "Gentleman Dan" Kane. Once he had been in a game with Kane and had caught him palming a card. Pryor had jumped him, but Kane had quit cold, returned the Rio Kid his money.

Several citizens stood around Kane, who was talking with them.

"By golly, there's Tex O'Byrne, too," thought the Rio Kid, who knew most of the hard characters who preyed on the railroaders. "He's never far from Kane."

The giant cowboy was lounging in the shade, and half a dozen toughs were with him.

"Now what's up?" mused Pryor.

Major North rode over to him. His dark-faced Pawnee scouts, under Lieutenant Murie, waited on the edge of town for their chief.

"We've got to get back on the line, Bob. You comin'?"

"Not yet, Major. Thanks for the hand."

"Don't mention it. So long."

The lean, tall North swung his horse and headed for his scouts, to lead them back to guard the Union Pacific builders.

Bob Pryor strolled over to the veranda on which Dan Kane stood. Slouched at one end of the porch, he heard Kane saying:

"Let's see your papers, mister."

"Here yuh are — what'll yuh give me?" asked an eager settler.

"A hundred down and balance in six months," replied Gentleman Dan.

"Aw right. I'll take it."

The pioneer came down the steps, counting greenbacks.

"Sellin' yore land, mister?" the Rio Kid asked politely.

"Yep. Sold my farm and I'm headin' for other parts." The fever of speculation glowed in the settler's eyes as he hurried past Pryor. With that cash he would buy options at the new town site, and when the railroad came he was sure he would own a fortune.

"Oh, now, mister, it isn't worth that much," the Rio Kid heard Gentleman Dan say. "Remember, all I want to do is start a sheep ranch."

"Him work?" thought the astounded Pryor.

Something was up. He couldn't guess what, but Kane and Tex being on hand told him it was something crooked.

He walked back to where McClean and his folks had pushed into the crowd and were listening with eyes and ears wide. Seeing how the fever was spreading, the Rio Kid decided to interfere. These were good people, settlers and emigrants alike, and Kane was up to some dishonest game.

Pushing a way through, he got up on the wagon and raised his hand. Chickenhead Sims had run down and was mopping his pink face with a red bandanna.

"Folks," Pryor began, smiling at them, "yuh shouldn't go off half-cocked like this. Nobody knows where the railroad'll cross the Wood River 'cept General Dodge and a few of the high muckamucks. I can swear to that."

"Are yuh callin' me a liar?" demanded Sims, turning on him angrily.

48

"Nope," the Rio Kid replied coolly. "Just mistaken, mebbe. Surveyors cover sev'ral routes and the road picks the best one. Sometimes the way that looks hardest proves best. It might be here, and it might be Dogtooth Gap, and again it mightn't be either place. Calm down and think it over, 'fore yuh sell out yore holdin's."

From the corner of his eye he saw Tex O'Bryne start up and come over, his men at his spurs. Now he knew he was right.

"I accuse nobody," he drawled, "but it looks like a deep game. The U.P. don't like speculatin', 'cept for itself, and they keep shet about their real route. Any time they can change their routes and river crossin' by miles if they want to."

His words were like ice water cast upon the listeners. The more thoughtful began talking together in undertones.

McClean's party took the advice to heart.

Some Riverside people had already started for Dogtooth Gap, after trading their holdings to Kane. Others, like Chickenhead Sims, had the fever too badly to check themselves. Despite the sage warning given by Bob Pryor, a number of the settlers decided to move.

The Rio Kid got down off the wagon and headed for the town pump. He had a drink of water and looked up to see big Tex O'Byrne bearing down on him, trailed by several roughs. The giant Texan's beet-red face was scowling.

"Hey, you!" he snarled, laying a hand on the Rio Kid's shoulder and whipping him around. "I wanta talk to yuh."

The Rio Kid hit him in the teeth with the back of his hand.

"Yuh kin work yore ugly mouth without maulin' me, Tex," growled the Rio Kid.

"I'll have yore hide for that," snarled Tex, "and nail it to the fence!"

But he did not come at Pryor nor did he make a move for his guns.

The Rio Kid stood there, his reckless eyes laughing, daring Tex O'Byrne. Pryor's booted feet were spread wide in the mud that surrounded the town pump where the beaten earth was constantly being wetted down, and his Colts hung free and easy at his slim waist.

O'Byrne's gunmen, grouped to one side close at hand, waited for their leader to open the ball. But Tex did not.

He knew the Rio Kid, knew him to be a first-class gunfighter, a friend of Buffalo Bill and of other well known Frontier figures.

"Why can't yuh keep quiet?" Tex asked lamely, his pale eyes blinking. "What've we done that yuh horn in on us?"

"So I'm hornin' in on yuh," the Rio Kid took him up. "I figgered as much. Why not tell me yore game, Tex? Why's Gentleman Dan buyin' in lots here? Is he the one shovin' these folks off to Dogtooth Gap?"

Tex O'Byrne realized he had let something out of the bag and he gulped, his massive jaw working. He was not given to mental deception. Physical violence was his strong point.

"Shucks," he said, "that's nothin' to me. C'mon, boys."

He had decided not to tangle with the Rio Kid, whose reputation as a fighter had spread from the Rockies to St. Jo, from the Rio Grande to Dakota.

His great boots sucked in the gummy mire surrounding the town pump and with ill-concealed amusement the Rio Kid watched him plod away.

CHAPTER
SEVEN

To Keep the Devil Away

Jim Barringer had seen the Rio Kid slap O'Byrne, and was galloping over, while McClean and several of the Irish emigrants were also approaching, ready to help their friend. The Rio Kid looked down, and his quick eye, trained to pick out the tiniest signs on a trail, noted the "X" impression in the heel of Tex O'Byrne's large footprint.

"Now I wonder," he muttered, starting forward.

It was more than a hunch. The killer of Jim Barringer's father was a man with oversized feet, and a cross in the heel. O'Byrne answered that description, and while many superstitious individuals wore a cross of nails to keep the devil away, the coincidence of Tex O'Byrne also being here in Riverside, Barringer's home town was too striking not to arouse healthy suspicion.

"Oh Tex!" called the Rio Kid, as he hurried after the towering hulk of a man.

O'Byrne turned, pale-blue eyes narrowed.

"What yuh want?" he snapped.

"Tell yuh what I'll do, Tex," said the Rio Kid. "Yuh want me to leave town. I will if yuh kin beat me fair and square. Shoot yuh two rounds at a target."

"All right," agreed Tex. "What'll it be?"

"See that hitchin' post over there with the busted top? I'll put five bullets in the center within an inch of each other. Then it's yore turn."

He whipped out a Colt and let go, emptying the six-shooter faster than a man could count, hardly seeming to take aim. Splinters flew from the center of the narrow post. The Rio Kid turned to O'Byrne with a grin.

"Yore play, Tex," he said, as he broke his revolver, ejected the five empty shells, and pushed fresh ones in.

Tex O'Byrne drew a revolver, inlaid with mother-of-pearl, from his right-hand holster. He took more careful aim than the Rio Kid had, and more time. Finishing the round, he broke the gun and threw out the hot cases.

"Let's go take a look," he said. "I aimed over yore marks, Kid."

He started toward the post, his men after him. A shooting match was always a matter of intense interest on the Frontier. Quickly Bob Pryor picked up a couple of Tex's spent cartridge cases. Around the rim were marks left by the hammer, and they were identical with the ones on the cases which Jim Barringer had picked up by his father's body!

"What's goin' on, Bob?" asked Jim Barringer as he came up.

Tex and his friends were examining the grouping on the post.

"Hey, Rio Kid!" Tex called. "I think I done better on this one than you did. Look!"

"I've got the man who kilt yore father, Jim," Pryor said in a low voice.

Barringer gasped a curse. "How yuh know?"

"Here, look at these shells — and peek at his footprint in the mud by the pump. No doubt of it."

Barringer went pale under his tan. He paused to examine the big impressions near the pump, then ran over to where the Rio Kid confronted Tex O'Byrne.

"You murderin' devil!" Jim snarled. "You killed my father!"

"What the —" began Tex, but Bob Pryor broke in coldly:

"Yuh pinned it on yoreself, Tex. Why'd yuh shoot Jim's dad, back there on the plains? Yuh're under arrest for murder . . . Look out, Jim!"

For young Barringer had lunged in between the Rio Kid and the giant Texan. Tex's pistol was hanging in his hand, and he was as fast as a streak of light. The Rio Kid had only a slice of side at which to shoot as Barringer lashed out, hit O'Byrne in the flat nose, and Tex only fell back, his gun rising.

The two Colts seemed to blare together. Barringer was half turned by the bullet from O'Byrne's pistol. Tex did not shoot again but stood teetering, a wisp of gray smoke rising from his weapon.

Jim Barringer went down on one knee as blood spurted from under his torn shirt. But the Rio Kid's hastily thrown shot had paralyzed O'Byrne for the needed instant, ripping a deep crease across his ribs close to the heart.

54

Tex gasped for air, then he seemed about to fire again, but again Bob Pryor beat him to it. His shot hit Tex between his pale eyes and the giant fell as though struck by a poleax, landing on his broad back. As his big feet turned up, the light caught the metal nails in X formation in the heel.

"Look out for 'em, Kid, look out!"

That was Elsa McClean, crying a warning. She had seen O'Byrne's gunmen going for their guns while the Rio Kid had been occupied with Tex O'Byrne.

With no loss of precious instants, no jerky haste that might spoil the aim, Bob Pryor whirled on the gunmen, his Colt roaring. The nearest had his revolver rising to killing level, but the Rio Kid's bullet tore into his shoulder, dropping his hand.

The Rio Kid jumped for the big iron pump as a slug drilled air within an inch of him. His gun spoke even as he shifted. The sickening dull thud of lead in flesh told that he had disposed of another, who fell on his face, hands clawing at the wet dirt. Right in their faces the Rio Kid's Colt banged, deadly and invincible. Shaken, their bullets were wild, glancing off the pump or shrieking over Pryor.

One of them turned to run, cursing in panic, which streaked through their yellow hearts. They were killers but only when in a gang. Face to face with a fearless, accurate gunfighter like Bob Pryor they could not stand. So they turned to run, dashing across the plaza to their horses.

The Rio Kid, a smile on his lips, hurried them on with his bullets.

Something like a giant hornet hit the crown of his Stetson, nearly ripping the chin strap loose. The Rio Kid's hair was cut for him and the closeness of the bullet half-stunned him.

"Rifle!" he muttered, as he ducked down behind the pump, staring at the line of houses.

"Good fighting, Kid, good fighting!" cried Elsa, jumping up and down in excitement. "But, oh, poor Jim! He's killed!"

"Get behind yore wagon!" Pryor ordered, for Elsa was now bending over Barringer, fearless of the singing death about her.

"I will not!" she replied, cradling Jim's head in her arms.

Barringer was conscious, but bleeding and stunned from O'Byrne's bullet. The swift clash had occupied only a few seconds. Women, children and non-combatants were still headed for cover. No one knew the right and wrong of the argument yet.

Opposition to the Rio Kid, holding up his end all alone, was rapidly forming over at the building where Gentleman Dan Kane had been conducting his business. Kane was giving swift orders. Several more men of the same brand as those the Rio Kid had scattered appeared, guns in hand. The Rio Kid rapped some slugs at Gentleman Dan who hastily bobbed down behind the thick rail. A second rifle bullet nearly snuffed out the Rio Kid's candle as the long lead gashed his upper arm, ripped his shirt and tore along the ground for fifty yards before ricocheting from a flint rock and whistling on over the Wood River.

He saw the glint of light on the barrel that time. The rifle was thrust from a second-story window next door to the porch where Gentleman Dan Kane stood. Whipping out his full Colt, the Rio Kid broke the glass behind the rifle muzzle. The gun was hastily withdrawn and no more rifle shots came at him for the moment.

Gunmen were hurriedly leaping on their saddled mustangs. They meant to charge, and the Rio Kid heard Gentleman Dan ordering them out, although Kane himself stayed down behind shelter.

"Come back, Kid — over to the wagons!" roared Mike McClean. "We'll help ye."

Blood stained the Rio Kid's right hand, running from his arm wound. He saw some of the Irish emigrants hurrying Jim Barringer for shelter. Elsa was with them, but she was calling back to the Rio Kid. He followed to the big wagons. McClean's men there had their rifles loaded and ready.

Bullets sought the Rio Kid as horsemen charged across the square.

"Let 'em have a volley overhead!" McClean ordered.

His friends fired, rifles roaring steadily. The bullies of Tex O'Byrne and Gentleman Dan Kane did not like the menacing sound of the bullets all around them. For now the Rio Kid was no longer fighting them alone. Spurts of powder smoke rose from half a dozen prairie schooners. The leader of the gunmen attackers jerked his reins, swerved. His men piled up behind him. Cursing, they turned their horses and rode back. In only moments more the Rio Kid saw the black-clad Gentleman Dan on a big horse, leading the retreat out of Riverside. Gunmen and gambler were speeding across the plains, headed toward Junction City.

The Rio Kid laughed. He refilled his warm guns, and turned to Elsa, bent over Jim Barringer.

"Is Jim hurt bad?" he asked. "Let's have a look."

In the Civil War he had seen every kind of gunshot wound and could judge them. Barringer gritted his teeth, but did not groan when Pryor probed at the jagged wound in the young man's side.

"It'll heal," the Rio Kid said. "But he'll need to lie still and give it a chance for a few days. Fetch some fresh water from the pump, and let's lift him in the wagon. Jim, yuh'll be better off at home. Where do yuh live?"

"Three miles up the river." Barringer could speak, now that the shock was passing. "Gimme a drink, will yuh?"

Water was held to his lips. They hoisted him gently into the big McClean wagon, laying him out on a blanket. The Rio Kid climbed in, with Elsa, and set about making a temporary dressing for the bullet wound.

"Who's hurt?" a new voice asked from outside.

"Oh, hello, Grebe," the Rio Kid said, recognizing the Riverside hotelkeeper. "Jim Barringer got it, but it ain't bad."

"Looks like yuh're pinked yoreself," Grebe observed, indicating his bleeding arm.

"Let me see!" cried Elsa. "I'll wash it for you!"

"It's nothin' but a scratch."

But Elsa's gentle hands, tending his injury, pleased him and he let her wash it and bind it up. "Yuh're mighty good, Elsa," he told her, his voice low.

She looked up at him and smiled. "So are you. I never saw a man fight that way before."

Pryor was pleased. Elsa patted his arm and turned again to Barringer, who was watching them silently.

The Kid got down from the wagon,

"Take my advice, folks," the Rio Kid said to the crowd of citizens which had collected in the wake of Warren Grebe, "and hang on to yore land in these parts. The fact that Gentleman Dan Kane wants it means it's worth a lot."

"I reckon he's right," a townsman growled.

"I was goin' to move my hotel to Dogtooth," Grebe agreed, "but now I guess I'll stick here awhile."

"What'll we do, Mike?" inquired Dave Riley, a middle-aged Irish emigrant who was McClean's lieutenant.

Riley, heavy of face and body, was a married man whose three growing sons and two daughters had accompanied his buxom wife and himself. Courageous, the family of Riley, or they would not have ventured to leave their homeland. Here the women would back up their menfolk and the children loved excitement by nature, of which they had experienced more than their share since reaching this raw land.

"We'll camp in the square a day or two, till we find what's what," decided McClean, answering Riley. "That is, if it's agreeable."

"Yuh're welcome, mister," said a portly citizen. "I'm Phil Harris, the mayor here. Stay as long as yuh've a-mind to."

"Thank ye kindly. We've come a long way and a rest won't hurt any of us."

Harris frowned on the Rio Kid.

"Now look, you, I dunno the rights and wrongs of this gun battle yuh just pulled off. Yuh're mighty quick with them six-shooters —"

"He's the Rio Kid, Phil," broke in Barringer, "and straight as they come. Those hombres started it! That big devil murdered my father, Lew Miller and Ulman the other day!"

"They started it," cried Elsa. "I saw it all!"

"Ex-cuse me," Harris said, holding out his hand to Pryor. "I didn't savvy. Yuh're welcome, too, Rio Kid."

CHAPTER
EIGHT

Sad Home-coming

Quickly the emigrants began fraternizing with the towns-folks. The exodus from Riverside had been checked by the Rio Kid, although a few more wagons, including that of Chickenhead Sims, rolled south on the bumpy trail to Dogtooth Gap.

"Mac!" called Jim Barringer.

McClean looked in the back of the wagon, smiling at the somber young rancher.

"What is it, my boy?"

"I want to speak to yuh. There's a section of rich bottomland along the river. I think Ma would sell yuh — on yore own terms, and take as long as yuh need to pay. There's none better in Nebraska. Stay at the ranch till yuh get yore house up. My brother-in-law and me'll show yuh how to build."

"Why, that's great!" cried McClean. "But will yer mother . . . Well, s'pose we go and talk to her? It sounds like a foine opportunity to me. Don't it to you, Elsa?"

She looked up. After a time she nodded, but first she glanced at the Rio Kid, who was slouched against the wagon end, smoking. Pryor knew she was thinking that this flat land with it wearisome monotony did not stir her soul.

"I hate to think of tellin' Ma," he heard Barringer mutter. "It'll break her heart when she finds out 'bout Dad."

"We'll help you, Jim," Elsa said quickly. "Lie comfortable, that's a good boy."

Most of the emigrants preferred to remain in town where they felt safer.

"I'll see ye in a day or two, Riley," said McClean, as the wagon started to leave with the wounded young plainsmen.

"Say, mister, one of them fellers ain't dead yet," reported a scrawny-necked town youngster. "He's squirmin' and cussin'."

The Rio Kid walked back to the scene of battle. Tex O'Byrne was as dead as one of the nails in his bootheel that had betrayed him. A second gunman had died instantly. A third, however, a bearded man with deep-sunk eyes rolling in his ugly head, was still alive. He had not long to live, however, the Rio Kid found, as he squatted beside him. Bullets had drilled his vitals, and his beard was covered with bloody foam.

"Six thousand Sioux — they'll dry yore scalp — I'll get yuh for this — Rio Kid!"

His hate, his fury against the man who had started him on the last trail, spewed from his dying lips.

"Aw, yuh're talkin' nonsense," Pryor snarled, trying to lead the gunny on.

"Kane'll take yuh — chief's too smart — for yuh — Spotted Tail's got — six thousand — yuh skunk —"

"Kane don't savvy Spotted Tail," the Rio Kid growled. "Here, have a drink!"

He poured water between the gritted teeth, and the gunman's eyes widened. An eye for an eye and a tooth for a tooth was the motto on the Frontier.

"Chief's got — Sioux — in hand — kill yuh, torture yuh — burn yuh —" raved the dying killer.

"Yuh can't fool me," the Rio Kid prodded him. "Why'd anybody want to use the Sioux?"

"Railroad —" The dying gunman coughed, sighed as though punctured, and relaxed, his neck and body going limp.

The Rio Kid felt his heart. It had stopped beating.

Pryor looked up. McClean was on his wagon box, reins in hands. The big schooner creaked off, up the river road, headed for Barringer's.

The Rio Kid straightened up, whistled a few bars of

Said the big black charger to the little
   white mare,
The sergeant claims yore feed bill
   really ain't fair —

It was an Army song and Saber's favorite. When the dun heard it, he would come running.

Mounting, the Rio Kid waved his hand and swung after the wagon. Elsa rode inside, kneeling by Barringer, helping to ease the jolts for him.

The Rio Kid was deep in thought, trying to make something of the dying gunman's ravings. Gentleman Dan Kane and some friend of his, it seemed, were in touch with the Sioux. They could command Spotted Tail's warriors.

"I'll hafta find what their game is," the Rio Kid muttered.

As yet he had only this inkling of what that game was, or how great it loomed as an instrument that could spread grief and terror . . .

When the small party reached the Slanting B Ranch, Jim Barringer's home, young Barringer found his grievious duty even worse than he had anticipated, because his mother did not cry when the news of her husband's death was broken to her.

She was tall, and her hair that had been a warm dark-brown when she had come in a covered wagon with her man to the Indian-infested plains of Nebraska was gray. And her hands were red and harsh from work, the work she had done so cheerfully, raising her children and taking care of her husband.

Lines had touched her face, but it was still pleasing. Her daughter Elizabeth, Jim's sister, looked much as her mother had at the same age, slim and dark-eyed, but strong, a pioneer's wife. Bessy had been married for two years to Luke Norman, a good-natured, powerful young fellow who helped work the ranch. In season they hired several cowboys for whom the two women had to cook.

"He's dead," Sarah Barringer said dully, and that was all.

Jim, propped up in a chair, with Elsa at one side of him, and his brother-in-law at the other, saw something die in his mother's deep eyes. But she did not weep.

64

"I knew it," she said after a time. "I felt it."

But such Frontier women had strength, not only of body but of soul. Death was all about them, violent death, from guns, from the elements, from the Sioux. This they faced as they faced other problems.

Elsa's heart was touched. She went to Jim's mother and laid her hand on the older woman's.

"Please lie down now," she begged. "I'm going to fix you some tea."

Bessy was crying as if her heart would break, and her husband went to try to comfort her. The Rio Kid stood aside, his heart going out to them, but able to do nothing. Only time would help, and only the younger people at that. The wife could never regain what she had lost.

"Let Elsa take care of yuh, Ma," Jim Barringer pleaded. "For my sake."

"All right, son," his mother gave in, but first she saw to it that Jim was made comfortable in his bedroom.

The house was low of roof, the windows a bit narrow and poorly glassed. Most of it was made of sod bricks, though timber which had been imported to enlarge it, kept the worst of the rain out. A "soddy" was not, even at its best, a tight and comfortable place. In heavy rains dirt washed through the roof and drizzled down inside. The bricks often crumbled.

But the Barringers were better off than most of their neighbors. The pioneer father had been enterprising and had made money selling the cattle he raised. They had food, fuel for the fireplace and cooking, and good water.

The barn was a great dugout, bigger than the house, built into the lee side of a mound behind the home, which faced the flowing silver river. After digging a well into the little hill, bricks of sod had been piled and cemented to lengthen the walls. Boards and long logs stretched horizontally, with three feet of packed earth on them, made the roof.

It was a crude life and a hard one, but Jim Barringer looked on it as normal, for he had been born out here. He loved horses and cattle, dogs, of which they had a dozen — big-eared, ravenous hounds, always underfoot. The flats were home to him and he enjoyed speeding over them at breakneck pace on one of the fine-blooded mounts his father had bred. The flying rope to check a long-horned steer's rush, the exciting hunt for game, fishing for "cats" in the river, mush-and-molasses, jerked beef, chicory coffee, two feet of mud when it rained, terrific cold, constant wind, boiling summers — all these were the breath of familiar life to Jim Barringer.

He felt better the next morning, the shock of his wound having passed, for he was young and powerful. But he was sad at his father's death and at his mother's quiet grieving.

And yet something new, something more exciting than anything he had ever known had come to him. It was Elsa McClean, and he knew it. His eyes sought the low, narrow doorway, hoping she would soon be up. She had slept in his mother's room and he did not wish to disturb them.

66

Then the Rio Kid appeared in his door and laughed in at him.

"How yuh feelin', Jim?"

"Fine! I'm mighty obleeged to yuh for avengin' Dad, and for savin' me. Tex killed my father all right. That gun couldn't lie, and his footprint cinched it."

"We got the right man. And yet, Jim, I'm sort of sorry I didn't just down Tex. Though that kind won't usually talk."

"Why should yuh want him to talk? We savvy he killed Dad."

The Rio Kid shrugged. He did not want to trouble young Barringer with the speculations that were in his clever mind.

"As long as yuh're all set," he said, "I reckon I'll ride on back, Jim. I'm s'posed to be pardners with Buffalo Bill, furnishin' meat for the railroad."

Jim Barringer was sorry to see Pryor leave, in one respect, but in another he was relieved, although he tried to stifle that feeling because he knew it was jealousy. Elsa admired the Rio Kid and smiled upon him quite as often as she did on Jim Barringer. It was selfish, but Barringer was glad he was going to have a clear track for a time.

The Rio Kid was strolling off, his spurs jingling, when Elsa came out of Mrs. Barringer's room. She was fresh and sparkling in the morning light.

"I'll hafta leave for a while, Elsa," Pryor said to her, as he took her hand. "My pardners, Buffalo Bill and Celestino Mireles — he's usually with me — will be worryin'. Besides, I have somethin' to see to. But I'll be comin' back."

"Be sure to," Elsa said. "I'll miss you. It's hard to thank you for all you've done for us."

The Rio Kid bent over and said something Jim Barringer did not hear. Elsa flushed, then she laughed, tossing her coppery curls as she went to the fireplace and poured a pitcherful of warm water from the always steaming bucket.

Barringer groaned. It was not from physical pain, but Elsa heard and came hurrying to his side.

"Jim — are you all right?"

Barringer was ashamed of himself but heard himself saying:

"My side hurts somethin' awful, Elsa."

"Poor boy!" She was greatly distressed, for she had deep sympathy for the suffering, and was every ready to comfort.

The Rio Kid ducked through the low-hung doorway. He smiled and waved, and disappeared around the turn.

Shortly they heard the sound of clopping hoofs, and Elsa glanced out the narrow window.

"I like him," she said. "I never met a man like him before."

"He's a great feller," Barringer said generously.

Win or lose, young Jim Barringer would always be like that.

CHAPTER
NINE

The Great Warrior

Ruby fires marked the great camp of the Sioux. Low-throbbing war-drums called the fighting men of Chief Spotted Tail to the council.

The night was fine, with stars and a half moon overhead, while the constant west wind blew. Set at strategic points, up on the little isolated buttes that overlooked the plains, were Indians sentinels, so there was no chance of a surprise attack by any of Sherman's, Carr's or Custer's cavalry.

This was not a home camp of the mightiest and largest of the plains Indians, but a temporary hideout from which raids on the way stations, on the railroad camps and isolated settlements might be conducted. No squaws and no children were with the braves. Many of the women and children had been left in agency camps, or had retired to the foothills of the Rockies, in Wyoming and Montana.

Buffalo and deer hides served as rough shelters, as beds, on which were gayly colored blankets, provided by Indian agents on the promise of good behavior — a promise usually ignored when inconvenient. Over five hundred hand-picked warriors were with Spotted Tail.

Fifteen hundred hairy Indian mustangs were close at hand. Every brave had at least one good rifle, a pistol, knife and tomahawk. And this was but one division of the Sioux.

Angered by the white man's encroachment, and with much to be said for their case, the mighty Sioux had declared war. The Black Hills, their sanctuary, the home of the Great Spirit to them, had been violated. Their buffalo range, vital to livelihood, was being cut in two by the steel rails the whites relentlessly pushed across the hereditary country of the Dakotas.

Cheated in many instances by venal agents, and with their lands taken from them, the Sioux were fighting — in the only way they knew — by stealth, by trickery, by guerrilla warfare which gave no quarter. The war, that was to last for over ten bloody years, was on!

Isolated stage stations were raided, the inhabitants dragged out for torture or taken prisoners to be slaves of the Sioux. Small flag stops on the Union Pacific and Kansas Pacific were attacked, burned. Agents were scalped, stock stolen. Ranches and farmhouses, tiny settlements, travelers on the plains and in the hills, graders, engineers, track layers — all felt the fury of the Sioux.

They fought superbly, but they were doomed. No matter what the cost in life and property, no matter what it meant to the red barbarian, the civilization of the white man relentlessly pressed westward.

Now in their bivouac the Sioux warriors of Spotted Tail rested. Weird figures, with buffalo and cow horns attached to their heads, and with streaks of paint on

70

their fierce, high-boned copper faces were here. Braves wore breech-clouts and eagle feathers, carried shields made of layers of hide taken from the crotch of old buffalo bulls. Such shields would stop an ordinary bullet. Leggings, moccasins and belts were masterpieces of bead work, and, adding to the colorful barbaric picture, were tomahawks and shining guns that had been taken from the whites. And they could be off at a moment's notice, so swiftly that no cavalry could hope to keep up with them.

Sherman had twenty-five hundred soldiers in the west, strung along in the isolated posts for two thousand miles. The Sioux could muster six thousand elusive fighting braves.

About their fires, screened by the banks of the ravine in which they hid, the Indians were eating and drinking. They had cooked meat and were tearing it with their white teeth and strong hands, gulping it down with cool water from the little stream at the side of the camp.

In groups the Sioux made their meal. The low roll of drums — buffalo hide spread over hollowed logs — brought the sub-chiefs in. The great Spotted Tail, chief of all the Brule, a confidant of Sitting Bull and Gall.

Spotted Tail squatted, a handsome grizzly bearskin draped about his wide, copper shoulders, close to the upper end of the camp. He had a proud, dark face, the wide and high-boned face of the Sioux, the black eyes and curving eagle beak of his people. One sinewy hand rested on a powerful naked thigh, the other on the blood-encrusted hilt of his long scalping-knife stuck in the doeskin belt which also held a tomahawk and a fine Colt's six-shooter taken from some Frontier victim. A new Spencer seven-shooter lay within quick reach. He wore beautifully beaded boot-moccasins, and the claws of a gaint grizzly stuck out over his ears.

Here indeed was a great chief, a man of destiny.

"Bring the *wasichu* to me," he ordered one of his sub-chiefs in the guttural Sioux tongue.

Soon a white man was shoved up before Spotted Tail by three stalwart warriors.

"Spotted Tail!" the man cried. "I've been trying to get to you for a week! You *must* listen to me."

The interpreter, a half-Sioux, half-Mexican who had been born in an Indian village and educated at an agency mission school, translated. Spotted Tail replied.

"He says you are in a hurry. He calls you the 'Man Who Must.'"

"Tell him I'm here for his good as well as my own. I can show him where to pick up real loot, plenty of horses and guns!"

The narrow-eyed interpreter translated again while Spotted Tail listened, showing nothing of what he thought. After a time, he spoke. He waved a hand and there was majesty in his bearing.

"The Sioux are at war to the death with the *wasichu* — the white man. You are a *wasichu*. The *wasichu* has stolen everything the Sioux had — his land, his buffalo, his tepee and his squaw. Until the rivers of the great plains run blood instead of water the Sioux will fight."

72

The visitor listened impatiently until Spotted Tail finished his oration, a mixture of blood-curdling threats, pathos and humor dear to the Indian heart.

"I want to help the Sioux," insisted the white man. "Have your warriors attack and burn a village called Riverside — and a ranch near there, the Slanting B. That first, but there are other places as well. The Sioux may kill as many as they can."

Spotted Tail listened and thought it over. He glanced around at his taciturn sub-chiefs, and answered.

"He says he is too short of ammunition to strike a whole settlement."

"I'll supply plenty of that! Guns, too. I have three wagonloads waiting. I'll give valuable information about the whites."

Spotted Tail seemed favorably impressed. He spoke a word or two with his aides.

"Are there any troops near there?" he wished to know.

"No. Only patrols now and then. Tell him that I'll give the word when he's to attack. I'll see there's little resistance."

Spotted Tail finally agreed. There were minor details. He wanted tobacco, new clothes, and a stovepipe hat. The *wasichu* promised everything.

"I have some friends who, like me, love the Sioux," he said. "How will the Sioux know us?"

Through his interpreter Spotted Tail answered:

"Tell your friends to wear these eagle feathers, the tips dyed red, in their hats."

The caller accepted the feathers offered by Spotted Tail. He gave careful instructions, arranging for a signal that would tell the chief when to strike the settlement. Then he was escorted out of the ravine. Half a mile away a dozen white men awaited him, held by armed Sioux, and sweating in fright, waiting for the man they called Boss. Gentleman Dan Kane was one of them.

"Well?" quavered Gentleman Dan. "How long are these red devils going to hold us here, Boss? They took our guns and horses and they haven't been any too gentle."

"Everything's settled," crowed the Boss, triumph in his tone. "I talked with Spotted Tail. The Sioux will strike where we say. Inside of three days there won't be a man, woman or child livin' in Riverside!"

Their horses and guns were returned to them, and the warriors melted away into the darkness.

Mounting, they rode away. Gentleman Dan growled after a time. "Listen, Boss, will those red killers scalp kids and women, too? It seems to me they could run 'em out instead — some, anyway."

"Dry up! Yuh can't expect Indians to do anything but work in their own way. Besides, we ain't got much time. We stand to make millions if we act fast. If we don't, we're lost. I'd have had them fools out already if that cursed Rio Kid hadn't stopped it. If I ever get a crack at him! Anyhow, we've got to have Riverside and the ranch — you know that. The Sioux'll help all along the line."

"Just the same, woman and —"

"Shut up, I said. It's all settled."

74

CHAPTER
TEN

A Fight on the Plains

Passing over the flat plains, the Rio Kid was much annoyed when, after riding two hours from the Barringer's back toward Junction City, he spied a band of Sioux in war paint and feathers, obviously out looking for trouble. Riding with his usual trained caution, he had seen them before they saw him. Then he took to the cover of a small swale, until they were below the far-off wave drop of the plains to the south.

Saber, hidden in the split of the earth, and trained to keep quiet when ordered, was treated to some choice profanity as they waited, impatiently, for the Indians to pass.

"Things 've gone to pot for fair, Saber," murmured the Rio Kid. "The Sioux are shore out in earnest. Yuh can't ride a mile without bumpin' into a passel of the red devils."

Resuming his way, he had made but three miles when he spotted more warriors off to the south, hovering along the line of the Overland Trail.

"Shucks," he muttered. "We might as well lie up till it's dark."

He found a secure hiding place and, concealed in thick brush that filled the ravine, he napped. When the sun dropped behind the distant Rockies, he saddled up and once more started for the railroad camp. He kept going through the dark hours, pausing only to rest his horse and let the dun drink from a small stream.

When the grayness of dawn showed he knew he was not many miles from the graders, who worked out ahead of the track layers. He ought to run into Buffalo Bill Cody and Celestino, he thought. They would be out after beef when it was lighter.

"Mebbe the Sioux won't be so thick today, near camp," he thought. "I'll hafta warn North and the workmen to watch their hair!"

Cre-ak! Cre-ak! Cre-ak!

The squealing sound that reached him meant wagon wheels rolling on the Overland Trail, down to his right in the shallow valley of the Platte. He swung over. Whoever was on the Trail must be warned against the Sioux, who were pushing their rebellion into a full-fledged war.

Presently, from the top of one of the regular swells of the plain, he made out three large carts, about one hundred yards separating them from each other, following the river trail. They had canvas tops, and six mules pulled each one. They were heavily laden. The Rio Kid could tell that by the way the animals pulled, and by the way the wheels sunk in the dirt. White men were driving.

The Rio Kid spurred down to intercept the train. They must be warned against the swarming hostiles ahead. In such times a military escort was almost imperative for a cargo through. Perhaps, passing rail's-end in the night, they had escaped the attention of the authorities, who might not yet realize the seriousness of the situation on the plains.

He rode down a dry gap, hidden from the wagons until he was almost upon them. The first two had passed, and the third was already abreast of it as he pushed Saber out into the trail.

His sudden appearance at the side of the big wagon, for the drivers were deafened by the creaking of the enormous wheels and the cursing of the mule-skinner handling the reins, made the fellow on the Rio Kid's side nearly jump out of his hide. A whiskey bottle stood between them.

"Well, I'll be hornswoggled!" ejaculated the driver, jerking his long reins spasmodically. That pulled on the lead-mule's bit and the beast obediently stopped, fetching the other five to a halt. "Who in jumpin' —"

"S'posin' I was a Sioux huntin' yore hair," said the Rio Kid, with his infectious grin. "There's a thousand of 'em up ahead and —"

He broke off and the smile left his face, while his blue eyes narrowed.

He had recognized the rough-looking man at the driver's side as one of the gunmen with whom he had had the brush at Riverside the morning before! Suspicion seized upon him instantly. He had not seen any other travelers on the Trail, and decided that the Sioux uprising had frightened off small parties, who would not be allowed through without proper escort. The Pony Express men would tear through, whatever might come, some to be killed and scalped, but most of them to speed past too fast to be taken by the Indians. A man such as the Rio Kid or Buffalo Bill might chance it, trusting to superior horseflesh and guile to elude the savages. But never a small wagon train.

"What yuh doin' — sellin' whiskey to the Indians?" he growled and snatched at one of the tie-ropes holding on the cover. The knot came loose and jerked the section of tarpaulin off. He saw square wooden boxes, familiar to a soldier's eyes. Ammunition!

"So Kane's runnin' stuff to the Indians," he snapped. "General Dodge and General Sherman'll be mighty interested in this."

He jerked his reins, and the dun, with a snort, whipped around. The *cluck-cluck* of a cocking rifle had warned him, coming from the rear of the big prairie schooner. Then he caught the glint of the light on the brown-steel barrel thrust almost point-blank in his face. He ducked as the rifle roared deafeningly. The Sharps sounded like a cannon.

With the speed of legerdemain, his right hand pulled at his Army Colt. His expert thumb caught the hammer spur as it rose and then lifted, letting the filed-trigger mechanism strike. The Colt barked, a treble echo to the mighty bellow of the buffalo gun. He was dazed, and burnt powder had stung his cheeks. His Stetson had been blasted off his head, torn to ribbons by the heavy charge. But his tingling scalp did not interfere with the coolness of his atuomatic motions.

His first .45 slug tore a neat hole in the canvas two inches from the rifle muzzle and the hairy hand steadying the barrel. A yell of pain came from inside the wagon and the Rio Kid's next bullet hit the man who fell forward, his head and broad shoulders pulled over by the weight of the Sharps.

The Kid's second shot struck between the man's shoulder and neck, killing him.

The Rio Kid threw his revolver around, for the two on the driver's box were down, guns already rising, torn from their side holster. The Rio Kid got the driver before the man got his Colt high enough to fire. A slug sped by his ear from the other side of the wagon, and Saber swore in mustang language as another one singed his mouse-colored hide.

"Down the line, Saber!" yelled the Rio Kid, and spurted to the rear of the wagon.

The two leading wagons had stopped, and a dozen men leaped from them, with rifles and pistols.

"Get him!" he heard them shouting. "It's the Rio Kid!"

A volley sought him but the wagon bulk protected him, and his own fast lead made them think again. They slowed, hunting cover.

The fellow who had been on the box with the mule-skinner was pressed close to the high, mud-laden wheel on the other side. The Rio Kid saw the scared look in his eyes as he jumped the swift dun out from behind the prairie schooner, his Colt blaring. He heard the whistle of two bullets, but he was moving all the time, then his own shots took effect and the man slumped against the wheel, groaning, clinging to the spokes.

"I reckon I need a Stetson — the sun's goin' to be hot," he grunted. Streaking up, he snatched the big gray hat from the wounded gunman as he pivoted.

Roars of fury, gunshots, came from the men from the other two wagons. The bullets were too thick for comfort about his ears, and Bob Pryor touched the dun, spurring away from the back of the wagon. The schooner gave him some protection until he had ridden several hundred yards where the gunmen could see him clearly. Low over the dun, he rattled the enemy with more Colt slugs. Then the range was too long for them to reach him, and he was driving full-tilt over the rising and falling plains.

"I'll shore talk to Gentleman Dan Kane on this matter," he muttered hotly. "Supplyin' ammunition to the hostile Indians is a criminal offense. The Army and Railroad'll want to take a hand."

After a fast run into the rising sun, he came upon signs of the railroad builders. The first grading had been roughly done and wheel marks showed. Topping a rise, he saw one of the deep cuts through an isolated butte, a characteristic of the plains region. The graders had dug straight through it.

He headed the mouse-colored dun into this narrow cut, its clay sides not yet smoothed out. The smoke he could see did not alarm him for the graders would have a fire. At the eastern end of the cut he could see a grader's camp with pickaxes, shovels and tools lying around. Men, too, in rough corduroys and jeans — which was strange, for it was not a meal hour.

"Jumpin' horntoads!" he muttered. "The Sioux have been here!"

He jerked the dun's reins. He had ridden right into a trap! Realizing it, he acted instantly. Off guard because of the proximity of the graders, he had grown careless for an instant. A harsh command from over his head told him that that second's lapse of vigilance meant he was done.

A line of rifles was trained upon him and behind each one he saw the eagle feather and glittering black eyes of a Sioux brave. A dozen warriors sprang up, starting for him as he pivoted Saber to make a run for it and die fighting, rather than by slow torture at the savages' hands.

But more of them had closed in from his rear.

The situation looked hopeless. There seemed to be no escape. The dun was trembling violently, hating the smell of the Indians, which he had failed to scent before because of the wind at their back, and the taint of the wood smoke in the air.

Bob Pryor was starting to draw his pistol for a final fight to the death when a huge Sioux in a chief's eagle-feather head-dress, carrying a brand-new Army rifle and belted across his naked body with double slings of ammunition, threw up both arms and roared a command in the Indian tongue.

At the sudden change in the demeanor of the savages the Rio Kid left his revolver in its holster. No shots came at him, and the huge chief ran up to him and raised his hand high in salute. He spoke in the Sioux guttural, and the rifles were withdrawn, while the

81

braves relaxed, although they crowded around the man on the dun.

Saber bit and kicked out at them, showing his hatred. "Take it easy, Saber," warned the Kind.

He was astounded, and, suspecting some trick, listened while the Sioux made him a speech of welcome. Blinking in his surprise but keeping a poker face, he tried to see what would happen if he moved. The braves melted from the dun's path, the chief trotting alongside and talking to him. He heard "Spotted Tail," several times, then they were out on the flats once more, the graders' camp at hand.

Most of the forty workmen were dead, their heads bloody messes from Sioux scalping-knives. Arrows still stuck in their flesh, although the Indians would retrieve them before they left. Several dying victims were staked out in the sun, suffering slow torture. The clothing and belongings of the graders had been taken, and it was plain the Sioux had come upon the railroaders while their guns had been piled, and some careless foreman had not had a watch out.

The Rio Kid knew he could do nothing now to save any of them. For he had seen this sort of thing before. This was not the first grading party the Sioux had surprised.

"The Man Who Must" was being mentioned by the sub-chief. Evidently he was one of Spotted Tail's allies. The Indian invited the Rio Kid to mount and share the loot, but he shook his head.

He did not dare say much, for fear of breaking the strange spell.

Indian mustangs cropped the curling buffalo grass, awaiting their riders. The Sioux would not remain long here but, their horrible work done, would be off before any pursuit could begin. Seeing that the man on the dun wished to go on, the chief drew back, raised his hand in farewell, and the Rio Kid wanting to pinch himself to see if he were dreaming, trotted the dun on, making it slow, although it was difficult not to hurry. He knew too much of Indian methods with a captive not to worry. Death was far preferable to falling into hostile Sioux hands.

Sioux braves, streaked with war paint, impressive in their gorgeous paraphernalia, and armed to the teeth with first-class weapons squatted all along his path, tasting the contents of the lunch-boxes of the dead graders.

"Redfeather," he heard several of them grunt, in Soux. "Let him go — Redfeather."

CHAPTER
ELEVEN

The Chronicler

Keeping his steady pace, the Rio Kid finally dropped beyond the rise where the future railroad was already graded. Once he was below the horizon, though, he dug in his spurs and swept on like the wind.

"Saber, I must be dreamin'," he muttered, glancing back over his shoulder. "The Sioux musta got religion . . . No, they didn't show them graders any mercy! 'Redfeather' — now what in tarnation is that!"

He took off the Stetson he had snatched from the head of the gunman at the wagon train and looked at it. Sure enough it had a feather stuck in the band, a real eagle feather, the tip dyed a bright crimson. "Come to think of it," he told himself, getting an inkling of what must have saved him, "all the men I seen at them wagons wore a red-tipped feather in their hats."

The red feather, then, must be a badge known to all the Sioux asthe mark of a friend.

"They wasn't Brules, either," he thought. "But they know Spotted Tail, of course. I reckon I'll keep yuh, Redfeather! I feel a heap safer."

Five miles on, he saw the bell-shaped funnel of the work-train, and hundreds of men were laying tracks. In good stretches as much as two miles a day would be put down and spiked, after the graders were through. Flat cars carrying rails, ties — for all wood had to be transported to the treeless plains — were hitched to the smoking engine. The walking boss was bellowing his orders to the swarming gangs of laborers — Irishmen, Poles, Germans, Slovaks, and mixed blood strains. They wore muddied, old overalls and corduroys, battered felt hats, cow boots or laced shoes.

Hairy faces were lifted for a glance at the lathered horse and handsome rider, as the Rio Kid slid to a stop near the boss. Steam swished from the little engine. The clang of steel, the cursing of men, rose on the warm air. It was a familiar enough sight to the Rio Kid, who had been shooting buffalo to feed these men for some weeks.

"Hey, boss," he sang out, to the giant Irishman in charge. "If yuh want yore gradin' done yuh better call out the Army! They're all dead up there! The Sioux caught 'em."

Profanity streamed into the air. The bearded boss cursed the Sioux, the railroad, everything else he could think of.

"Rifles, guns!" he bellowed, face beet-red.

"Won't do yuh any good," the Kid told him. "The Sioux'll be gone 'fore yuh can make it. But keep a sharp eye out. They're thick as fleas today."

He waved, and rode on toward Junction City.

Celestino Mireles was in camp, watching for him, when he pulled into the town. Saloons and gambling places were quiet, awaiting the return of the laborers to liven up for the evening.

He swung off the dun as his young Mexican partner ran quickly to his side.

"General" — to Mireles, the Rio Kid would always be his "General" — "I theenk you nevair come back! I keel buffalo but ze Sioux are like leaf on ze tree!"

"Good boy, Celestino. Where's Buffalo Bill?"

"Under zat wagon, takin' a siesta."

The hunters had finished for the day and Buffalo Bill was taking an earned rest. Pryor saw to his horse, unsaddling and rubbing Saber down, then picketing him where he could graze, before attending to his own wants. While he was finishing up a plate of beans and buffalo tongue, there was a stir and some soldiers, among them Major Frank North, two other white officers and a couple of dozen Pawnee scouts rode in.

The Rio Kid went to meet his friend, the major. North's grim face was spattered with blood when he greeted the Rio Kid. There had been a fight. A couple of the Pawnees carried flesh wounds, but they also carried fresh Sioux scalps.

"The Sioux burnt a way station thirty miles back on the line," North informed. He was breathing with difficulty, for he suffered from asthma at times. "Scalped the agent and pulled up some rails. We chased 'em and came up with one band."

"They're up ahead, too," reported Bob Pryor. He quickly described what he had run into. "I want to talk to General Dodge, Major. There's somethin' fishy goin' on."

86

"Dodge went to Washington to see President Johnson, I believe," said North. "I'll hafta start out again after that party of Indians yuh run into, Kid."

He gave some orders in Pawnee to his men, then went over to the water buckets for a drink. As he bent over, a heavy-set man in a dark-blue suit and a brown derby came hurrying from a saloon across the muddy street. He had deep-set, baggy eyes and a walrus mustache and as he covered the rough ground between North and himself he rolled with a heavy limp that gave him the appearance of intoxication.

"Say, Major — you're Major North, the White Chief of the Pawnees, ain't you?" he cried.

"Yeah, I'm Frank North," the tall officer replied, turning to look down into the eager man's face.

The fellow was older than the Rio Kid and North, looked like an Easterner, and yet he had the mark of the outdoors on him, tanned by the sun and wind.

"My name's Judson," he said. "I'm a writer and work under the pen-name of Ned Buntline. Maybe you've hard tell of me."

The Rio Kid watched with amusement as Ned Buntline buttonholed Frank North, the acme of modesty and diffidence. But he recognized this stranger's name instantly, because in the latter part of the War, the Rio Kid, then Captain Robert Pryor of Grant's Army of the Potomac, had been loaned several paper-backed novels about the sea, wild tales that cost a dime apiece and were designed for boys chiefly. These had carried Ned Buntline's signature.

"You're growing famous, Major," Buntline went on rapidly. "I've heard tell of you back East and lots of folks have, from the papers. Now, all you need to do is tell me a few stories of your experiences and I'll fix them up and sell them, and we'll make a lot of money together. I'm suck of writing sea stuff and all the kids are howlin' for Westerns today. I want a real Indian fighter, and you fill the bill!"

He whipped out a pencil and a pad, and blinked up into North's face. Ned Buntline was ready to satisfy the demands of his public.

His real name was Elmo Z. C. Judson, and he had started writing sea stories while at Annapolis. Once he had written a six-hundred-page novel in sixty-two hours, hardly pausing to eat or rest. His own life was a series of riots and gunfights, duels, prisons, and wars, every sort of adventure.

He wrote with terrific speed and already had a great name among his widespread public.

"Oh, shucks, Buntline," North growled. "You don't want a man like me. Say, Kid, here's someone would like to write you up. Meet Ned Buntline, says he's a writer. This is Bob Pryor, the Rio Kid, who's had a lot more big times than I ever did."

It gave North the willies to think of having attention fixed upon himself as a hero of the plains.

Ned Buntline sized up the Rio Kid, and seemed satisfied. "I need stories, Rio Kid," he said. "Have you had any adventures lately? Why not let me write you up?"

The Rio Kid laughed. But Frank North was stealing away, and Pryor had a great deal on his mind.

"Mebbe later, Buntline," he said good-naturedly. "I got business to see to now, but I'll tell yuh what I'll do. Come over here and I'll introduce yuh to my pardner, Buffalo Bill Cody."

"'Buffalo Bill — Buffalo Bill,'" repeated Buntline. His deep-set eyes lighted. "Why, that's a great name for a Western hero! Where is he, this Buffalo Bill?"

Buntline rolled with his unsteady limp after the lithe Rio Kid, who was trailing Major North.

"I've steered him onto Cody," the Rio Kid whispered to his tall Army friend. "Let's see what Bill says!"

They located Buffalo Bill sleeping under a big wagon.

"Wake up, Bill," the Kid said, nudging Cody with his boot toe. "Yuh're goin' to be made immortal!"

"He'll fill the bill for you, Buntline," Major North said solemnly, enjoying the spectacle as the eager writer helped pull Buffalo Bill, still half asleep, from under his shelter.

"What in —" growled Cody, rubbing the drowsiness from his eyes, staring at the man. He stood up, the tall, handsome plainsman.

"I'm Ned Buntline, the writer," the limping man said. "I want to talk to you."

Buffalo Bill shrugged, for there was no way he could guess that this man was to make his name a synonym for the brave plains scout and Indian fighter and an inspiration to the youth of the universe. Buntline had tight hold of him and would not let go, while the Rio

Kid and Major North, glad to slip away unnoticed, went rapidly along the other side of the wagon.

North smiled as they heard Cody saying helplessly:

"Yeah, I killed plenty of Indians, mister. But —"

"You're the very man I'm after," broke in the author. "Come over here where we can talk in peace."

Captain Luther North, the major's younger brother, came riding up with more Pawnees, in from the fight to the east, where the Sioux had raided the station. "Lute" was not as tall as his more famous brother but he was a splendid scout and soldier.

"Things are bad, Frank," he reported gravely, swinging off his charger that was sweated and caked with muck. He wore Army blue, a wide-sweeping cavalry Stetson, a saber, and high black boots. "We need reinforcements to strike out far after 'em."

Frank North nodded. He could muster two hundred Pawnees in his battalion. General W. T. Sherman, in command of the Western district, had about twenty-five hundred soldiers but they were scattered in isolated posts throughout the vast region.

"Now look, Major," Bob Pryor said earnestly, "those ammunition wagons ought to be got after pronto. There's enough bullets in 'em to supply the Sioux for weeks."

"You're right, Kid. And just as soon as I can whip my men into shape I'm startin'."

"I'll go along. I got a bone to pick with a man in the camp; see yuh soon."

The Rio Kid meant to lose no time in facing Gentleman Dan Kane and the men who worked with the sleek gambler. He did not know what the entire game was, but he could take a flying guess, from what had happened at Riverside. The words of the dying gunman there, the red feather and the connection between the ammunition for the Sioux and Kane's aides, made him certain that Kane's gang was trying to cash in somehow on the tremendous inflation in land values that would be brought about by the coming of the railroad.

"Elsa and her folks may be in trouble," he mused, "if I don't act pronto. I don't fancy the way things are shapin' up."

He liked McClean and the other emigrants in the train he had helped. And the folks of Riverside could not be overlooked. But primarily it was Elsa who was on his mind. Because of her he was considering, if she would have him, giving up his wild, untrammeled existence. He was young, despite his long war record, for he had enlisted in his 'teens and risen rapidly because of his bravery and ability.

Elsa McClean had attracted him from the first. Her bright nature and happy voice, her all-embracing sympathy for those in misery, made her wonderful to him. She was young, beautiful, spirited, the kind of girl who would mean more to a man than the world itself.

"She'd love Texas," he thought, "or the Rockies. She seems to be that kind of a girl."

CHAPTER
TWELVE

Surrounded

Shrugging, the Rio Kid shut away his dreams, for practical matters claimed all his attention. Spurs clinking, he strolled along the muddy road toward the small office of the Union Pacific which was in a three-car train on a siding. Passing a nearby shack he heard his friend Buffalo Bill saying: "Why, yeah, I did stab him when he come at me, but what else was a body to do?"

And, though the Rio Kid did not know it, Ned Buntline already was writing:

The red devil, a giant in stature, launched himself through the air straight at Buffalo Bill, knife flashing in the warm air of the plains, as the intrepid scout braced himself for the shock. Armed but with a knife, his warm six-shooter emptied of bullets, Buffalo Bill looked death in the eye as —

"Aw shucks," growled Cody, and the Rio Kid laughed.

He had not seen Gentleman Dan Kane and his bully boys since pulling into Junction City. No doubt Kane was keeping out of sight. The Rio Kid swung onto the car platform, and looked through. Engineers sat at draughting boards in the first car, and he could see busy clerks in the next section.

"I been told General Dodge is in Washington," he said to a man busy at the nearest table, "but I want to see whatever boss was left in charge, with him away. I'm Bob Pryor, the Rio Kid, and I got somethin' important to report to the company."

A stout man with a semi-bald head got up from an armchair near the center of the car and came along the aisle.

"I'll talk to him, Carter," he said to the clerk, fixing the Rio Kid with cool gray eyes.

He wore a woolen shirt, open at the throat, whipcord trousers tucked into fine, high-laced engineer's boots, and his sleeves were rolled up. He exuded importance.

"I'm a camp hunter — work with Buffalo Bill Cody," the Rio Kid told him.

"And you have something of importance to tell me?"

"That depends who yuh are," the Rio Kid replied.

"That's all right, sir. I'm George Olliphant, General Dodge's assistant on the section. Come outside where we can talk."

He smiled and nodded, and the Rio Kid followed him out.

"What I wanted to talk to the General about," the Rio Kid began, "is that I've run into some queer doin's at the town of Riverside. It has to do with the railroad, and I figgered yuh'd be interested in stoppin' it."

"Certainly. What is it?"

"There's a slick gambler named Gentleman Dan Kane and a gang of his, who're after that town. I don't know whether or not the rails will strike there, but Kane seems to think so. He's after all the land in the vicinity, and is steerin' folks to Dogtooth Gap, south of Riverside."

"There's a good deal of that going on," observed Olliphant.

"Yeah, but this is diff'rent. Kane and his bunch are supplyin' the Sioux with ammunition and guns and eggin' 'em on to attack. That depresses land values, and folks'll sell cheap, if they don't move off altogether, them that are left alive. The Sioux are bad enough without bein' encouraged."

"You're right, Pryor," Olliphant said. "We're grateful to you for telling us this. The railroad is most certainly interested. I'll put our detectives on it at once. Kane ought to be arrested."

"I figger on havin' more evidence in a few days," promised the Rio Kid. "I'm ridin' out now with Major North and his Pawnees. We aim on scoutin' Riverside."

"Fine. Be sure to report to me when you get back. The general will be most interested. In the meantime, we'll keep this quiet until we have all the evidence against Kane and his bunch."

George Olliphant grasped the Rio Kid's hand, thanked him again and swung back to the car step, while the Rio Kid went away to prepare to ride on a dangerous scouting trip with Major North and his Pawnees.

Buffalo Bill, unable to shake off the tenacious Ned Buntline, wanted to go along.

"Take me with you," begged the writer.

"Ask the major," Cody replied. "I don't care if yuh lose yore hair, Buntline."

"Can you ride a horse?" inquired North, when the request was put to him.

"I can try," Buntline said stoutly . . .

By the next dawn they were far out on the plains, headed west. The Rio Kid and two big Pawnee scouts, Cody and North, were strung out in advance, smelling the way for the battalion. Not a sign of the Sioux moving did they see, however, and when they reached the spot where the wagons had been encountered by the Rio Kid, they were gone.

Following the wheel tracks, they crossed the Platte, and saw that the wagons had been driven on for some miles, then stopped. The clever scouts read the sign of what had occurred. The drivers had met a large band of Sioux Indians and unloaded. Then the carts had been driven off, making a big curve that led toward Riverside.

In military formation, the battalion moved on, their Spencer carbines burnished and ready. The dark faces of the Pawnees were set. They seemed to smell trouble ahead.

The Rio Kid rode near Major Frank North, out in the van. Suddenly, as they topped one of the endless crests in the great plains, the Rio Kid cried out in astonishment, pointing ahead.

"Good gravy, Major! Do you see what I see!"

Two Pawnee advance scouts were tearing back at full-tilt, madly flogging their mustangs, howling a warning.

Across the plains stretched great lines of Sioux warriors in full battle array, the sunlight glinting on rifles and pistols, on long knives and tomahawks. Barbarous plumes waved in the air, and gay-colored ribbons flew from tails and manes of the ponies, and from lance-standards.

"There's a couple of thousand of 'em!" exclaimed North.

He snapped commands and his bugler blew blasts on his trumpet. The main squadrons of the Pawnees rapidly took up a defensive formation. North, Cody and the Rio Kid could see that the Sioux held the plains. They were lined out in half-moon curves, and if the wings kept speeding up they would envelop the battalion in open ground.

The White Chief of the Pawnees was a brave man, a fearless soldier, but he was also a good strategist. To fight such a large number without cover would be suicide. On the other hand, to retreat before the Indians was usually fatal.

"Let's get back to the battalion," he said quietly.

The Rio Kid, Buffalo Bill, and Ned Buntline, whose eyes were as wide as cartwheels at sight of the Sioux, were shooting at the approaching foe. The bugle was blowing again, retailing Major North's orders.

"We'll make for that prairie grove we passed awhile ago," North informed.

They fell back on the battalion, lined out in open fighting order. Spencers began cracking and the guns of the Sioux replied. For a time it seemed that the Indians would succeed in their circling movement, but the Rio

Kid took one flank, and Buffalo Bill the other. Their accurate fire slowed the sub-chiefs who sought to pull their braves around too fast.

That peculiar roaring, yet indefinite sound made up of the clash of arms, the cries of fighting men and animals, rose to the sky. Major North called in two of his big Pawnees. "Sky Chief — Tall Bear!" he ordered. "Ride as fast as you can to Fort Kearny. Tell the commander-in-chief there we've engaged two thousand Sioux!"

The two scouts swung their fast horses and streaked away.

"Queer, they don't seem eager to engage," North remarked to the Rio Kid, as they fell swiftly back on the rough stretch which the major had ticketed in his keen mind when they had passed it a short time before. "Looks as though we'd come up on them."

"Mebbe they're on their way to Riverside," growled Pryor.

The rear guard had reached the priarie grove, several hundred yards long and fifty or sixty across, an isolated islet of woods in the vast ocean of the plains. It was typical of the region, a patch of trees and rocks growing in strange and solitary splendor. No one knew why the great plains were so bare of timber. Some said it was because, for generations, the Indians had burned them off to provide fodder for the buffalo. But, here and there, such a grove was encountered.

"Dismount!" roared Major North, and the bugle shrilled the order.

The horses were dragged into the grove, pushed close together among the rocks and trees. The swift, lithe Pawnees, grabbing Spencers and ammunition belts and boxes, squirmed into little depressions behind stones or tree trunks and began shooting.

The van of the Sioux had come up within four hundred yards but at the terrific, accurate fire of the expert marksmen in the prairie grove, they felt the stinging death. Brave after brave was hit, many falling from their mustangs, to be picked up by friends. Then, unable to stand that kind of punishment, they drew off, howling and shooting at the grove.

North had not lost a man although one had been cut by a nearly-spent rifle ball. But they were not through with the Sioux. The hostile Indians had ridden around to form a complete circle of the grove, at a safe distance.

"I reckon we're here, boys," remarked the Rio Kid dryly.

He loaded his rifle afresh, placed some bullets handy and took out the makin's, to fix himself a smoke. Ned Buntline was lying flat on his stomach, close to Buffalo Bill.

"Say, Bill," he asked the handsome scout, "this ain't a joke you boys fixed up to play on me, is it?"

"Listen," growled Cody, "if yuh want to find out, Ned, just take a pasear out there and ask one of them Injuns for a light!"

CHAPTER
THIRTEEN

Captives

On the second day after his injury, Jim Barringer was up. He limped a little and to ride hurt him, but his clean life, natural strength and youth quickly put him back on his feet. Many a man might have been abed a week or two with such a wound.

His whole family loved Elsa McClean. To Jim's delight, his mother took to the girl from the start. His sister was charmed to have a companion so near her own age and one who had seen something of the world and come from far across the sea, a girl who loved pretty clothes and the things girls fancied.

Michael McClean, strong as a bull, knew how to handle animals and work around a farm or ranch. As soon as Jim was able to fork a horse, they visited the section of bottomland where Jim thought the McCleans might settle. Michael and Elsa rode in a buckboard, while Jim walked his horse beside them.

Arrived at the spot, McClean got down on his hands and knees and dug out chunks of the soil with his stubby fingers, feeling it, chuckling.

In the Wood River, was water for living and for irrigation purposes. A shallow valley here would make an ideal site for house and barn, near the eroded dull-gray bluffs rising on the opposite bank of the stream. All about stretched the short-grassed, mighty flats, once considered as useless, but now recognized as a great corn and wheat-growing section.

"Yuh like it, Elsa?" inquired Jim eagerly, watching her.

"Ye-es — yes, Jim. It's splendid." There was doubt in her voice, but she smiled up at him as they stood side by side. "I could plant some trees later, couldn't I?"

"Shore, Elsa. This dirt'll grow anything. Havin' no timber to clear off the fields'll make it easier for yore dad. Yuh can build a nice soddy. We'll help yuh."

He could not see the emptiness of it, as could one who was accustomed to broken, wooded country. To Jim Barringer this was home, and its monotony familiar juice. A sodhouse was as satisfactory as any abode, to a man who was outdoors all the time. Buffalo chips were good enough for fuel.

He took Elsa's hand and she did not draw away but smiled into his eyes. The air was fresh and warm, and they were young, with the sun slanting upon them.

Michael McClean came back, grinning widely.

"Jim, if your mither'll take the cash I have and notes for the balance, it'll be a great day for the McCleans to have this wonderful land."

"I'm shore Ma and Sis'll be glad to let yuh take up here, Mac," Jim Barringer said. "And we'll get on great together. Sometimes ranches and farms don't mix but it don't hafta be so. We'll string some fences so's to keep the steers out of yore crops."

100

"Ye're a foine lad, Jimmy, my boy. What say we drive on to the village and tell my friends? Mayhap I can help 'em settle not too far off so we'll all be neighbors like."

"C'mon," agreed Barringer. "We can make it and be home by dark . . ."

As soon as they came up on the crest of the rise bounding the little depression they could see Riverside before them across the flat. Smoke was in the sky, dark smoke from the fires of buffalo chips that curled out of chimneys. Soon they were among the emigrants on the plaza, while Dave Riley, Pat Corrigan and the restcame crowding eagerly about the McCleans, singing out cheerful greetings.

"We've had an offer of some good lands, Mac," Riley reported, "and we mean to go have a look at 'em in the mornin'."

"Where be they?" inquired McClean.

"Southward, along the river."

"I'd sort of hoped we'd settle near each other," McClean told his friends.

"Yuh won't find nothin' better, Riley," a tall man in jack-boots growled. "The railroad's goin' to run thirty miles south of here!"

For the first time Barringer noticed the fellow who wore a heavy leather coat and a gray Stetson with a large eagle feather stuck in the band. The tip of the feather was dyed crimson. He had a bearded face, skin red and rough, and he wore guns.

Jim Barringer decided he was a tough.

Warren Grebe was sitting on a wagon tree, listening, and the mayor stood near, while townspeople mingled with the Irish emigrants.

"Yuh'll be wiser, folks," drawled Barringer, "to let me help yuh out on settlin'. Nobody savvies this country any better'n I do. And what the Rio Kid says of the railroad is right. Yuh can't tell yet where she'll come."

The agent who was trying to sell land sections bristled.

"Say, looka here, young feller. Yuh got a big mush on yuh, haven't yuh — hornin' in on other men's business?"

It looked like a fight, but Warren Grebe jumped up, face reddening, and interposed.

"Jim's the man to listen to, friends," he declared. "He's right."

He scowled at the agent, who, seeing that opposition was building up, shrugged and hastily backed off, deciding that discretion was the better part of valor. Crossing the square, he entered a small house a couple of doors down from Grebe's "Riverside Hotel," a two-story structure with a bar-window front.

Warren Grebe grinned, slapped Jim on the back.

"That'll hold him. He's been hangin' 'round a couple days, him and his pards, tryin' to trade and buy land here. Folks, there's no better man than Jim Barringer in these parts. Jim, how's yore wound today?"

"Middlin', Warren, middlin'. Thanks for hornin' in for me . . . I'm goin' to sell the McCleans that dip 'tween here and the ranch."

"It's a good spot for a farm." Grebe nodded. "Come over and have a drink 'fore yuh go on back, Jim. Any of you people are always welcome at my place."

Elsa smiled on him and he touched his hat. McClean was speaking with his friends who had come over with him from the Emerald Isle. They had come to feel a clannish interest in one another, but now they must split up and each seek his own destiny in the great new land across the sea. Some would till the soil, others would work at various necessary tasks in building the nation. There were those among them who would grow rich, while others would face tragedy, poverty and death. But when their children were grown they would no longer be foreigners. They would come from the great melting pot — Americans!

The sun, over the dreary bluffs of the Wood River, was taking on a reddish hue. The day was well along, and soon they must be on their way home. Jim Barringer strolled over to Miller's general store.

"I'll buy Elsa a present," he thought.

Sunbonnets hung from a stretched wire and a dark-blue one took his eye. He bought it and, with the package under his arm, went out onto the board sidewalk. Warren Grebe hailed him from the hotel.

"Come in and wet yore whistle, Jimmy," he invited.

"All right," Barringer said. "But I can't stay long, Warren."

Grebe set up drinks, and toasted:

"To that pretty little Irish girl. She's a beauty!"

Jim drank the toast willingly, for already Elsa occupied his thoughts to the exclusion of everything else.

Suddenly half a dozen men came in the front door of the saloon. One of them was the land agent with the red-tipped feather in his Stetson. The men came pushing close to Barringer.

"Here, what's the idea?" Grebe said angrily.

He threw himself toward the revolver which he kept on the shelf of the bar. Colts clicked and a couple of the men had him covered. In the mirror Barringer could see the weapons rise behind him, and so could Grebe, who was forced to freeze and raise his hands.

"Keep quiet, both of yuh," the so-called agent snarled, "or we'll blow yuh over the floor."

"What d'yuh want?" Grebe demanded truculently.

Barringer could not go for his pistol. The muzzle of a revolver was in his back ribs, then someone snatched his gun from the holster.

"Don't say a word," the agent snarled, "or we'll kill yuh! We mean it. Start walkin' to the back — pronto!"

Grebe and Barringer, with the steady Colts trained on their vitals, walked through the rear door and out into Tin Can Alley, filled with debris, piles of tin cans and garbage.

"Fetch 'em along," the man said, after he had seen no one was in sight.

The two captives were forced along and, three doors down, swung into the back entry of the small house into which the land agent had gone a little earlier. Barringer, watching for a chance to escape, had no idea what it was all about, but he knew he could not chance a break now. He would be dead before he made fifty feet.

He and Grebe were shoved into a back room in which was one window looking out on a blank sod wall of the house next door. At a square table on which was a bottle of ink, some white papers, several glasses and a half-empty bottle of whiskey, sat Gentleman Dan Kane, the gambler.

Grebe was furious. He cursed his captors, growling, and one shoved him roughly to the wall.

Kane turned cold eyes upon the prisoners.

"So here you are," he said. "You've interfered with me, both of you, but I'll give you one more chance. Trade or sell your land holdings to me and you'll be turned loose."

Grebe laughed derisively. "Why, yuh dirty killer, yuh must be loco!"

"Well, Barringer, what say you?" Kane asked eyeing the young rancher.

"The same as Grebe," Jim growled. "Yuh must be crazy to try such stuff. Yuh can't get away with it."

"We'll see about that. Tie 'em up, boys."

Grene swore, and pulling his arm free, struck out at the man who blocked him, starting for the door. At the same moment Barringer sought to make his escape but was roughly slashed with a Colt sight, his temple cut. He went down on one knee as the toughs piled upon him.

Grebe was down, too, and they tied his hands and ankles, stuffing a bandanna in his cursing mouth. Barringer, too, was trussed up, then both were dragged into a small, dark chamber across the narrow hall and locked in.

After a time, as the sun went down and the light left the alley outside until their prison was in twilight, Barringer heard Grebe saying in a muffled voice: "Jim, I got my gag half off! Rubbed it off on the wall. Try it."

Barringer rolled over. His wound hurt, but he was able to wipe the gag down by repeatedly drawing it against the rough boards. Splinters cut his chin and nose but after a time he worked the bandanna far enough off to speak.

"Warren, what in thunder do them fools think they're doin'?" he mumbled. "Shall we yell for help?"

"Nobody'd hear us back here. They'd just come runnin' in on us."

Their wrists were fastened behind them and the tight rawhide cords had been pre-shrunk in salt water. It was impossible to loosen them by rubbing.

"They figger on scaring us into signin' over our property to 'em," Grebe said in a low voice. "I'm goin' to do it, Jim. If they're that dumb, mebbe they'll let us go once we do. Why, the deeds won't be no good! We can both swear they was signed under a gun!"

"That's so," agreed Barringer. "Anyhow, I only own a third of the Slantin' B. Why didn't we think of that afore?"

"Too excited, I reckon."

Grebe banged his heels, trussed together, on the floor. This brought Gentleman Dan Kane and several of his men. Kane looked in on them, a lighted candle flickering in his and.

"Well? What do you want?"

106

"I'll sign what yuh want," Jim said quickly. "Untie my hands."

"Me, too," agreed Grebe.

They took Barringer first, alone, back into the room across the hall. His wrists were loosened and he was given a stiff drink of whiskey. Then he blithely signed all the papers which Gentlelman Dan Kane put before him, knowing they would have no legal hold since they were signed under duress. They refastened his wrists behind him, very tight, and started to gag him once more.

"What in tarnation's the idea, Kane?" he cried, trying to fight them off. "Yuh said yuh'd let me go free if I done what yuh ordered."

"Dry up," snapped Kane. "Gag him, Tiny."

"Help —" began Barringer, but he was stopped almost instantly. Once more helpless and dumb, he was dragged back into the little dark prison room.

In the yellow flickering candlelight he rolled his eyes at Warren Grebe, trying to warn him not to sign. Grebe was puzzled as they led him away. The doors were bolted and locked but after a time Barringer heard a muffled yell, some thuds, and finally dragging noises in the corridor.

Grebe was not brought back, and the hours went on interminably.

CHAPTER
FOURTEEN

Savage Death

Dragging hours passed as young Jim Barringer lay stiff, with the cords cutting off his circulation. His wound ached almost unbearably. Finally the bolt was once more drawn and in came Gentleman Dan Kane. He was alone, and he had been drinking heavily, as attested by his unsteady walk, flushed face and bloodshot eyes. The candle shook in his hand, the shadows jumping in exaggerated frenzy on the wall. He closed the door behind him and leaned against it for a minute, looking at Jim Barringer.

"It must be after midnight," thought Jim. "Poor Elsa — what'll she think? They must've hunted me, and if they go home and tell Ma, she'll be . . . Now what's Kane figger on doin'?"

For the gambler had deliberately set the candlestick on the floor, and was coming toward him.

When Gentleman Dan stood over Barringer, he pulled out a knife with a stag-horn handle and a blade twelve inches in length. The steel was as sharp as a razor and gleamed in the light.

Barringer stared up into Kane's working face. The gambler's eyes were wide as saucers and he was biting his lip.

"Stop looking at me like that!" gasped Kane.

He raised the knife over Barringer and his hand tightened on the handle. Barringer could see the knuckles whiten.

"He's goin' to kill me," he thought, but sought to face it with a man's courage.

He watched Kane coolly, staring straight into the shoe-button eyes of Gentleman Dan. Kane had started the knife's downward descent, but as Barringer stared at him he shuddered, gulping.

"I can't do it — not in cold blood," he muttered. He kicked Barringer in the ribs, furious at him because he, Kane, hadn't the nerve to kill him.

Then he went out, and locked the door. It was two hours before the bolt slid again, and Kane staggered into the room, the knife in his hand. He was wildly excited, filled with red-eye.

Again he bent over Jim Barringer, the long weapon pointed at the young rancher's vitals.

Barringer believed his time had surely come now. Kane appeared worked up to killing point. But once more Gentleman Dan shuddered, swore, and threw down his knife.

"I — I'm not made for it!" he choked.

He walked unsteadily from the room. And all Jim Barringer could do was wonder how long it would be before Gentleman Dan would be able to gain enough nerve for the job . . .

Night had fallen over the prairie grove, and the faint rustlings of the many men jammed into the small area, the uneasy movements of horses' hoofs and the beasts' heavy breathings, pervaded the still-warm air which the wind was sweeping over the plains.

They had eaten cold rations while the hordes of Sioux, from a respectful distance, howled and sent in shots that did no harm. Now it was chiefly a question of water with the besieged battalion. The canteens would hold the men for three or even four days if sparingly used, but the horses must be sacrificed if reinforcements did not arrive quickly.

Buffalo Bill Cody, Major North, the Rio Kid, Lieutenant James Murie and Lute North, squatted together in a compact group to talk over strategy. Stars twinkled, but now and then a cloud shadow scudded with windspeed over the dark earth. The moon was not yet up. Ned Buntline, living intead of writing a story, lay near at hand, with Celestino Mireles and sub-officers of the Pawnee battalion silently listening.

"How long yuh reckon it'll take Carr to get help to us?" asked Cody.

"Oh, my scouts'll make the Fort in ten hours, if they didn't run into anything unusual," replied Major North. "But comin' back the troops'll be slower. I should say a day-and-a-half if nothin' goes sour."

"We're safe here," a staff officer declared. "We can hold out twice as long as that."

Frank North grunted in agreement. "It may keep 'em close and give the troops a chance to close," he said.

The Rio Kid was thinking in a different vein. He had Elsa and her friends on his mind.

"Major," he said, "those Injuns were on their way toward Riverside when we run onto their heels. If yuh'll give me permission, I'll try to snake through their lines 'fore the moon comes up and give warnin' to the settlements."

"It's a mighty dangerous job, Kid," North drawled. "I wouldn't want to try it and I wouldn't ask one of my Pawnees to do it unless it was life and death."

"I figger this is," Pryor insisted. "Can I go?"

"Shore," North agreed. "Yuh're not under military orders, Bob. Do as yuh've a mind to."

"I don't want to do anything to endanger yore command."

"Forget it. Wish yuh luck."

Mireles muttered, wishing to go along, but the Rio Kid knew he must travel alone. Cody would have gone, but Pryor refused to let anyone else make such an attempt. The Sioux, thick as autumn leaves, were alert and clever. They would be watching for scouts trying to snake through their lines.

Behind the rises glowed the redness of fires made of buffalo chips by the Sioux, and these lighted areas must somehow be avoided, although they made a full circle about the prairie grove.

The Rio Kid removed his heavy boots and replaced them with soft moccasins. Any leather might creak, so he thrust his pistols into his waistband and stowed spare ammunition in his pockets. He left his Stetson behind, too, binding his hair with a strip of cloth. But even as he made his preparations he knew that if the

Sioux caught him the lingering death he would suffer would be unthinkable.

As a boy on the Rio Grande he had learned to creep through the dry, crackly mesquite without making a sound, and had there met and outwitted the Apaches, the cruelest and most fiendish of Indians. As a scout in the Civil War, he had become even more expert, learning to pass through enemy pickets. On the Frontier this ability had been kept to its keenest edge.

"If they watch it'll be on our rear, Major," he said. "S'pose yuh make a little diversion that way while I get started?"

Mireles pressed his hand, anxious for his trail-mate. Buffalo Bill touched his shoulder without a word. Then the Rio Kid flattened on his belly and, keeping in the shadow of a tree cast from the grove, began inching out. Over on the opposite flank Major North began rattling some dry branches.

It was inch by inch for hundreds of yards. The scudding cloud shadows were a help. Close to the line of fires, the Rio Kid moved even more slowly, only when his straining ears, eyes and other senses, of touch, of feeling, of smell, told him he might chance it. He was hunting for a gap which must be shadowed enough for his own faint shadow to pass through.

As for a horse, he must try to steal one from the Indians without alarming the great army of Sioux, or else trust to his powerful legs in a run for it.

"Queer," he thought suddenly after a long wait.

He was up on the line of the fire circle. Red, smoky air surrounded him and still he had not heard, seen or

112

sensed the foe. An indefinite feeling, some instict or developed sixth sense, troubled him. He slowly raised his head from the dirt and looked to the left, to the right, ahead. No sleeping forms, no alert sentinels.

Suspicion turned to certainty. It was like jabbing out at what was thought to be a solid wall, to find nothing but thin air. What the Rio Kid realized was just as startling. The cunning Sioux had departed!

He rose higher, inviting attack. But none of the red enemies were left. The Sioux had evaporated.

Pryor leaped to his feet, and started around the ring. There was nothing to show the Indians had been there except the smoldering little heaps of black chips. He ran back full-tilt for the grove, singing out to Major North and his friends.

"They've gone, Major!" he cried. "They musta had a big job on hand to have let us out thisaway. I'm ridin' for the Slantin' B and Riverside!"

Major North snapped commands. The Sioux, they figured, had three hours start on them, long enough to devastate a town.

North ordered two scouts back to connect with the relieving troops from Fort Kearny. The Pawnees were always ready to go, and within three minutes the prairie grove was empty, and the Rio Kid, attired in his paraphernalia again, had slapped the saddle on Saber and was galloping for Riverside.

Buffalo Bill and Mireles rode with him. Ned Buntline was slower and stayed with the main body of the troops. With Elsa McClean on his mind, the Rio Kid rode low over his saddle, peering out at the windy darkness of the flats across which he raced, crooning to the mouse-colored dun, a shadow in the night. Saber was glad to run. The fleet, lanky horse, never matched by any other runner the Rio Kid had ever known, actually flew over the plains, leaving even Buffalo Bill behind.

Hour after hour the Rio Kid raced toward the Wood River. All the others had dropped far behind. The damp coolness of the new day was on his cheek as he glanced back, and the first lightening showed as a faint streak in the sky behind him.

This was the favored hour for Indian attack. Then, ahead and to his right, he caught a red glow over the plains, and he knew it came from the site of the Slanting B, the Barringer place. Spurs roweled the panting dun, and the Rio Kid's teeth gritted.

An hour later he was nearer and the light over the plains was now a gray, so that he could see for a mile. Smoldering ruins, the acrid-burning damp logs and wood, furniture, wagons, leather, stood before his widened eyes. Two figures, stripped naked and looking like arrow-cushions, lay sprawled in the yard. The sod bricks of the house and barn would not burn, but the wood parts did and the Sioux had poured kerosene on the buildings, made a great bonfire. The Slanting B was a horrible mass of death and destruction.

"Elsa!" he muttered, hitting the ground.

Examination told him that the two dead in view were Mrs. Barringer and Luke Norman, Jim's brother-in-law. But the red-hot, caved-in ruins of the house could not be searched for the others. If they were inside they were dead, at any rate, for no one could live in there, even had the Sioux spared them.

"Carried off — or mebbe burned alive in their beds!" he gasped.

Icy rage cooled the horror in his soul. Revenge remained. And the people in Riverside —

As the wind ceased for an instant, he heard firing break out south on the Wood, the site of the settlement. A moment later he was in leather, spurring that way, guns ready.

Tearing up, he found that the Sioux were in the square, attacking the Irish emigrants. All was confusion as guns blared from the wagons, from the buildings. There was no orderly defense.

Lithe, painted Indians were everywhere, screeching in triumph. Torches had been set to several wooden structures and flames were licking up. The Rio Kid, gun going, drove into the savages with a fury that nothing save a death bullet could check. His Colts roared, and every slug killed or wounded a Sioux.

They melted before him, firing hastily, but though he felt the nip of lead in half a dozen places he was traveling fast and was through before they could gang up on him. A scalped man lay near the central fire of the camp where the emigrants were fighting from their wagons.

Scattered resistance went on throughout Riverside, as the Rio Kid, firing point-blank into two giant Dakotas, with Saber lashing out, cracking skulls with his sharp hoofs, biting at red shoulders, tore in. He seized the upright post of the nearest prairie schooner, jumped off, and roared:

"Run, Saber — run!"

The dun kept going, zigzagging, fighting his way through the surprised Sioux, stung by hasty bullets but not stopped.

Dave Riley greeted him. "Howdy, Bob! It looks bad." The big man squatted at the rear of his wagon, trying to shield his wife and children who cowered down in front.

Blood was running from a gash in his cheek.

The Rio Kid's pistols were booming, clearing the Sioux out of the little wagon circle. Red bodies sprawled, one with every accurate crackle of Bob Pryor's guns. Over the settlement hung the horror of a massacre, about to be consummated.

Alone, the Rio Kid could only fight to the death with the Irish. Then suddenly came the notes of an Army bugle sounding the charge. With Major Frank North, in the van, followed by Buffalo Bill and Mireles, the Pawnee scouts with guns going, came sweeping upon the town. They were strung out in a line and every one was an expert marksman.

The Rio Kid could see, as he peered from a slit in the heavy canvas top of the prairie schooner, several white men, evidently fraternizing and fighting with the Sioux down the plaza. As one white man turned Pryor saw an eagle feather tipped with crimson in his hat. All the other white men wore such feathers. The Rio Kid also wore one. It had saved him when he had ridden into an ambush. But, coming in town as he had, attacking them, the braves had fought back. In the confusion, perhaps they had failed to see the feather.

"Lend me yore Sharps, Riley," he growled. "Here, use my Colt for a minute."

He set the big rifle on the wagon rib brace and took aim. It roared and the traitor with the red feather fell from his horse and sprawled in the dirt.

CHAPTER
FIFTEEN

The Retreat

Mainly through the fighting might of the Rio Kid the little space inside the wagons had been cleared, save for the twitching forms of dead and dying Sioux. And as North's battalion swept in, magnificent soldiers every one, delighting in the hand-to-hand struggle, the attackers fell back, leaping on their mustangs.

Trained troops were not the opponents the elusive, shrewd Sioux wished to encounter. North's sudden appearance in the dawn had come as a surprise, for the Indians, sweeping upon Riverside after devastating the Slanting B, had not been as well guarded as usual.

Before they could rally in force, urged by their chiefs and by the renegade whites scattered through the town, North and his battalion were protected as they fought by the various structures around the square. Cool and accurate, the Pawnees picked off sub-chiefs, and the leading braves. The rattle of arms rose, punctuated by the screams of wounded horses, by the cries of the wounded.

"Where's Elsa?" the Rio Kid demanded hoarsely, fearing to hear the answer. "Was she out at the Slantin' B, Riley?"

"Yeah, she was," Riley answered.

A Pawnee bugler blew a shrill note right in Pryor's ear, then Cody, Mireles, Ned Buntline and a troop of the fighting Pawnees surrounded the wagons.

'H'yah, boys!" the Rio Kid sang out. "They're on their way!"

It was true. The surprised Sioux who had believed they had the town to themselves, did not like the arrival of the Pawnees. North's troopers were dismounting, taking to clever strategic points of defense, and firing accurately into their blood enemies, the Sioux.

Down into the river guttered the Sioux, melting past the houses on their fleet, shaggy mustangs. The traitor whites went with them, and the Rio Kid, jumping from Riley's wagon, saw Gentleman Dan Kane spurt out of a house down the square, jump on a big white horse, and quirt after his cronies.

"Say, Bob," cried Riley, "I —"

"I'll be with yuh in a jiffy," called Pryor, already dashing out.

He whistled shrilly, "Said the Big Black Charger," and the dun presently trotted up to him, blood streaming from his hide, where Indian slugs had hit. Pryor hit leather and started after Kane, but Gentleman Dan was going like the wind, and disappeared among the retreating Indians. By the time the Rio Kid reached the other end of the town, Kane was safe, and a heavy volley from the hundreds of guns ahead roared about Pryor.

It was sure death to follow farther, so the Rio Kid swung back. In the town, the Pawnees were in triumphant possession. They were creeping out, and in the fresh morning light the scalping knives flashed, making a quick circle around the roots of Sioux locks. The major's bugle ordered fire to cease as the Sioux left the settlement and fell back along the river.

As the terrific excitement of the battle left him suddenly, Bob Pryor grew weak. He was bleeding from several wounds and Elsa's fate seemed sure. He dismounted by the pump, and began drinking, and throwing water on his cuts. Saber was thirstily sucking up liquid from the trough.

North and his Pawnees did not pursue the enemy. There were too many of them to engage in the open. Already Spotted Tail, whom they could see in the distance, was rallying his braves, and a long line of warriors rode out to encircle the settlement.

Citizens began to emerge from their homes. Several had died, and others were wounded, but the majority had been saved by the arrival of Bob Pryor and North's Pawnees. The mayor came up.

" 'Twas a close thing, gents," he gasped. "Another half hour and there wouldn'ta been a man of us left alive! We were teetotally surprised. We had two sentries out, but they were both stabbed to death 'fore the attack opened!"

Someone tugged at the Rio Kid's arm. He turned, his eyes dark-shadowed with the anguish inside his heart. It was Riley, McClean's lieutenant.

"Say, Bob, you asked 'bout Elsa McClean. She was out at Barringer's ranch but she come into town yesterday afternoon with Mike and the young lad.

120

McClean and her are over there in Devlin's wagon. Spent the night —"

The Rio Kid rushed from him.

"He's an impetuous young feller," Riley grunted, shaking his head.

The Rio Kid found the Devlin schooner filled with women and children. The men were out, their warm guns in hand, staring at the dead Sioux in the enclosure.

"Elsa — Elsa McClean!" cried Pryor.

There she was, her face pale and her eyes full of deepest misery. He held up his arms and she was lifted down. She put her arms about him and began to cry.

"Elsa — I thought the Sioux had yuh," he murmured, stroking her head. "They burnt the Slantin' B and massacred the folks —"

She gave a terrible gasp, and her eyes were streaming with tears. Her small body shook with her sobs and the Rio Kid could only hold her in his arms.

"Oh, the poor boy, the poor boy!" she was saying. "His mother — his sister — his father —"

Pryor held her tightly, his handsome face drawn into grim lines.

"What happened, Elsa?" He saw McClean coming toward them. "Yore dad's here, and yuh're safe. Where's Jim? How is it yuh chanced to be in town and not at the ranch?"

"We — we come in yesterday," she told him, fighting for control. Tears streaked her pale face, and her copper-red curls were dampened by them around her temples. "Jim, Dad and I. We were to go back before dark, Bob, but Jim didn't come to us, and we kept waiting for him till it was too late. Then we all hunted but he'd dropped out of sight. I don't know where the poor fellow is . . . Ah, his mother's gone, too, now!"

She fell once more into a fit of sobbing but presently, as he held her close, it subsided and she regained some control.

Fire fighters were throwing buckets from a line to the pump on the blazes. Howls and long shots came from the Sioux, strung about the town. The wounded were being cared for, and the settlers, grateful at the deliverance brought by the Rio Kid and the Pawnee battalion, quickly pulled themselves together. Elsa was so shaken that Pryor carried her to Devlin's wagon, and left her with the women, to be watched over and comforted.

The mystery of Jim Barringer's disappearance had struck the Rio Kid forcibly. Questioning McClean and the others he learned how Jim had dropped out of sight as though the earth had swallowed him up.

He had bought a sunbonnet at the general store, and someone had seen him go into Grebe's saloon. From there the trail stopped, for Warren Grebe had evaporated just as Jim had.

When Bob Pryor entered the Frontier hotel, people were standing around in there, talking about the Sioux attack, comparing narrow escapes. But Grebe and Barringer were not among them. The Rio Kid passed on through to Tin Can Alley, where firemen volunteers were throwing buckets of water passed along a human

122

line on the smoldering back wall of a small house a few doors down.

"Someone's in there, boys!" he heard a man cry. "I just heard him moan!"

Bob Pryor took in the smoke-filled back hallway, the red of licking flames burning the wooden panels. He ran between the building walls and came to a window which he smashed out with his gun butt. Hot air hit him, but the worst of the fire was in the hall, and he climbed in.

He felt the feverish breath of the blaze and acrid smoke caught at his eyes and throat, but there on the floor lay a trussed figure, with a bandanna half wiped off his bleeding face, eyes rolling. It was young Jim Barringer, feet and wrists secured with rawhide strips. The Rio Kid picked him up, carried him to the window. He was retching from the smoke, as he passed Jim out to willing hands.

"Grebe — I think — he's in there, too," croaked Barringer. "Gentleman Dan Kane wanted to kill me — but lost his nerve."

The Rio Kid had not seen the hotel keeper in the room where he had found Barringer. Not fancying any closer acquaintance with that smoky heat, he hurried to the front and went in that way. Others helped him but though they searched every room they could enter, they found no trace of Warren Grebe.

"Mebbe he was in that other back room," a citizen growled glumly. "If so, he's toasted to a fare-ye-well."

The Rio Kid had had enough of the smoke. The terrific fight and the long hours of strain before it,

123

reacted sharply as the worst of it was over. He dragged across the plaza, after the men carrying Barringer. Elsa came running from the wagons with a happy cry as she found that Jim wasn't killed, and instantly took charge of the young frontiersman.

Exhausted, the Rio Kid rolled in a blanket under a wagon and was asleep by the time he had closed his eyes . . .

He awoke refreshed, although his wounds were stiff and he was burning with thirst. By the sun he knew it must be near noon, and all around him were the wagon train folks and citizens of Riverside.

A new note, a fresh stir, was in the air.

Buffalo Bill Cody and Celestino Mireles slouched near him, watching out for him. Ned Buntline, Major North and his Pawnees were close at hand, and the Rio Kid sat up, reaching for a bucket of water the Mexcian had brought. He drank in great gulps. Feeling better, he began rolling a smoke.

"What's up?" he demanded.

"The Sioux faded away an hour ago," Cody grunted. "I reckon that's what!"

He swept his long arm in the direction by which they had ridden to save the town.

An army bugle was blowing the advance, a familiar sound to the Rio Kid. The notes never failed to stir him, and never failed to excite Saber, who would answer such a call day or night. The dun came over to him, stamping impatiently, pulling at his sleeve with his teeth, trying to make him get into action.

"That cayuse is a devil horse," remarked Buffalo Bill. "His mother musta been a mule."

Saber nipped at Cody's hand as the scout reached to pat him.

"Easy, boy," the Rio Kid soothed. "They'll be here soon."

Half an hour later the advance guard of the cavalry rode into Riverside, boys in blue with black Stetsons, the yellow stripe of the cavalry down the side seams of their trousers, tunics shining with brass buttons, high black boots catching the gleam of the golden sun. Spencer carbines were ready for action and the troopers debouched into the square, in command of a cavalry captain who saluted as Major North strode to greet him.

"General Carr's compliments, Major," the officer reported, "and he says he had your message and will be up within two hours."

The main force of the cavalry, three battalions of well armed, trained troopers, arrived on time. General Eugene A. Carr, the bluff, bearded commander-in-chief of the Fifth Cavalry, Border fighters and railroad guardians, approached. Golden epaulets sat on his heavy shoulders, and a cigar was gripped in his white teeth as he conferred with Frank North.

The two Pawnees sent in by North before the Sioux had treed them in the prairie grove had made a swift ride. Carr had been at Fort Kearny with a command, about to march, and had been able to start to relieve North at once. The major's second message had turned Carr toward Riverside, and the Sioux watchers, far out on the plains, had smoke-signaled warnings back to their friends who had instantly decamped, unwilling to face trained troops in pitched battle.

CHAPTER
SIXTEEN

Reward

For his meeting with the commanding officer, the Rio Kid spruced up as fast as he could. As he crossed the square to pay his compliments to Major-general Carr, a fine soldier and veteran fighting man, the rear guard and stragglers came into the town. A stretcher was brought up. A man lying on it was covered to the face with a blanket. The stretcher was set down in the shade of a big wagon.

"Pryor! Pryor!" the man on the stretcher was calling weakly.

He turned, to recognize Warren Grebe, the hotel-keeper.

"Why, Grebe! Glad to see yuh. Are yuh hurt bad? Barringer thought they'd kilt yuh."

He squatted by the weakened man. A bullet crease was visible, starting at Grebe's forehead and passing into the blood-clotted hair.

"We picked him up out on the plains," a trooper told the Rio Kid. "There were some Sioux near him but they run when they seen us. You a friend of his?"

"Shore. Grebe, what happened to yuh?"

"Is — is Jim all right?" gasped Warren Grebe.

"Yeah," the Rio Kid answered. "Gentleman Dan Kane and his gang tied him up, forced him to sign over his ranch to 'em, and then Kane tried to kill him but I reckon he lost his nerve. That's what Barringer figgers, anyways."

"They had me, too," Grebe whispered. His weak hand gingerly sought the wound in his head. "I managed to get my hands loose — rubbed the cords on a nail till one frayed through — then I finally untied my ankles. But as I was startin' out the winder, the Sioux hit the town and I got a slug in the head. One of Kane's men run in and seen me goin' out. Next thing I knowed I was joggin' along, slung across a hoss and tied up again. Couple of Kane's hombres and some Sioux braves were around, so I played possum. They were goin' to stake me on an anthill but when Carr's troopers rode over the crest they all run. I was lucky, I reckon."

"Yuh shore was," agreed Pryor. "We'll hafta arrest Kane, soon as possible. He's keepin' the Sioux stirred up and aimin' 'em this way."

"It's the railroad, I reckon — that's what I figger," Grebe said hoarsely.

"That's it exactly. Take care of yoreself, Grebe. Purty soon we'll have this business cleared up."

He nodded, leaving Grebe to the ministrations of the regimental surgeon.

General Carr's eyes twinkled as he shook hands with Captain Robert Pryor, whom he had known during the Civil War.

"Always in the thick of it, Cap'n, and still at it," he remarked.

"Yes, General. Trouble seems to hunt me."

Carr laughed. "Or you hunt it, Cap'n."

He introduced the Rio Kid to his staff officers. North waited, and plans were being discussed for the next move, for pursuit of the Sioux would be futile.

"I wish we could come up with them right," growled Carr. "The red devils are as slippery as so many eels. If we could locate their bivouac some dark night, now —"

Frank North shrugged. "It's mighty difficult, General. My Pawnees can usually smell 'em out but by the time any force gets up, the Sioux are on their way."

It was the same old problem of hide-and-seek, trying to catch the Indians so they would fight. But that was not in the Sioux strategy and they were not fools enough to buck trained troops. Hit-and-run, slash-and-fly were the clever Dakota tactics.

The Rio Kid, deciding he would put all he had into an attempt to arrest Gentleman Dan Kane and his gang of perfidious whites who were egging the Sioux on against Riverside and his friends of the wagon train, went to talk to Jim Barringer. Michael McClean came to greet him.

"We haven't told the boy yet about his mither and folks," McClean said in a low voice. "We thought we better wait till he's stronger. This all has laid him out for fair."

"That's right," agreed Pryor. "Wait till he can take it better."

He went to the wagon in which Barringer lay with Elsa tending him. Her face was pale but she was brave and much more placid than she had been. She smiled at the Rio Kid who looked in on Jim. Barringer tried to wave, but his hand was shaking.

"He'll be all right soon," Elsa reported. "We're mighty glad that he wasn't worse hurt."

Her eyes caught the Rio Kid's for a moment, and pity was strong in them for the young fellow suddenly bereft of all his dear ones by horrid massacre.

"I'm ridin' east, Elsa, in a short time," Pryor informed her gently. "Can I have a word with yuh 'fore I go?"

"Oh, yes," she said, and he lifted her down.

Out of earshot of the wounded man, the Rio Kid said:

"Of course yuh'll understand yuh're not to venture from the town, Elsa, you nor any of yore folks, till yuh hear from me. The troops'll no doubt stay here for a day or two. I'm headin' for Junction City."

She was looking up at him, her eyes filled with tears.

"I'll do as you say," she promised. "Oh, the poor boy! He keeps talking of his mother and his sister, as if they were still here. I can't face telling him."

The Rio Kid touched her hand. "Let yore father do it, Elsa. Jim's got to face it. I'll break it to him if yuh wish."

"You're a pillar of strength, Rio Kid — that's what you are. I wish I could tell you how I feel about you."

She suddenly stood on tiptoe and kissed his lips, then turned quickly back to the wagon and got in.

As on wings, the Rio Kid stalked back to his friends. He could still feel the warm, tingling caress of her lips, smell the perfume of her coppery hair.

130

"I'll smash this pronto," he thought, "then come for her. She's one woman in a million — no, in the world."

An hour later Buffalo Bill Cody, Celestino Mireles, Ned Buntline and the Rio Kid, on their fast horses, started for Junction City. The way was clear, for the troops had sent the Sioux flying from the Overland Trail. They made good time all through the afternoon and rode on under a starry sky, the wind at their backs.

Now and then they rested their horses, or had a sip of water. Before dawn they took two hours' nap, then resumed their swift journey toward the railroad camp. It was daylight when the Rio Kid, out several hundred yards smelling the way — though they had seen no signs at la of Indians — passed the deserted graders' camp and the cut where he had been surprised.

Nearly in, only a few more miles to go, he heard a hail from his left. Swinging in his leather, he saw a rider bearing in on him, holding up his hand in the plainsman's gesture of friendship. He was a white man, in the frontiersman's fringed buckskin, and soft-brimmed Stetson. Pearlhandled six-shooters showed in his belt and a rifle was carried in a sling under one long leg.

"It's Wild Bill Hickok!" the Rio Kid muttered, turned Saber.

Cody, Mireles and Buntline came hurrying up, to sing out greetings to the famous Frontier marshal and gunfighter, "Wild Bill," known all over the West as a great officer and fearless ace with a Colt. Tall, straight as an arrow, with long brown curls sweeping over his broad shoulders, with his aquiline nose, high brow and cheekbones like an Indian's, Wild Bill was as handsome a fellow as ever forked horse. He was, to the great plains country, what John Oakhurst had been to the California gold fields in the Fifties, a hero of godlike proportions.

Ned Buntline's jaw dropped as he found himself shaking hands with Hickok. James Butler, as Wild Bill's real name went, winked his eye when he heard that the worn-out man with the limp was a writer. But Buntline forgot his woes as he tried to question Hickok, only to be parried by jests.

"Say, looka here, Rio Kid," drawled Wild Bill, as they stretched their legs for the last lap to Junction City, "I'm an officer of the law, and out here huntin' some hoss thieves. 'Course this ain't in my jurisdiction less'n I got a warrant. But two thousand dollars is a lot of money, and what the devil have you took the owlhoot trail for at yore time of life?"

Bob Pryor was puzzled. He looked quickly at the shrewd Hickok's eyes to detect a jest but the marshal was as serious as fate.

"What yuh drivin' at, Hickok?" demanded Cody, an old friend of Wild Bill's.

"I ain't goin' to do nothin' about it," Wild Bill replied, lips pursing.

"Tell us what yuh savvy," ordered the Rio Kid.

In reply Hickok slowly extracted a folded white poster from his pocket, held it out to Bob Pryor, who read it with unbelieving eyes.

$2,000 *REWARD*
THE UNION PACIFIC RAILROAD COMPANY

132

WILL PAY THE ABOVE SUM TO THE PERSON OR PERSONS WHO ARREST OR CAUSE THE ARREST DEAD OR ALIVE, OF ROBERT PRYOR, ALIAS THE RIO KID, WANTED FOR MURDER AND HIGHWAY ROBBERY.
GENERAL GRENVILLE M. DODGE,
CHIEF ENG.

The Rio Kid could not believe his eyes. "Why, somebody's gone loco!" he snarled. "What's it for, Bill? Do yuh savvy?"

"Shore," replied Hickok. "A payroll of four thousand dollars was stole off the Union Pacific. It was after dark and they were puttin' it in envelopes, the manager and a paymaster, when a masked man jumped into the car and grabbed it. The paymaster went for a gun and the bandit shot him dead. The second hombre ducked behind the table and the outlaw missed him. But he described yuh to a T, Kid. Where were yuh the night of the fourteenth?"

Bob Pryor had to think back, although it was but a few days ago. So much had occurred that it seemed a long time.

"Why, I was headin' for Junction City, through the Sioux!" he cried. "They caught me but I got by because they thought I was a pard."

"Was anybody with yuh?" asked Hickok.

"No. I was alone."

"Shucks, we savvy Bob'd never do such a thing as that," Buffalo Bill said indignantly.

"I'm ridin' for Junction City," Bob Pryor snapped.

"Don't go off half-cocked, Kid," ordered Hickok. "Them laborers ain't worked for a couple of days, 'count of the Sioux bein' so thick, and they're pinin' for sport. They'll string yuh higher'n a kite. Every one of 'em will want that reward. Two thousand is a powerful big sum of money."

"He's right," declared Cody.

"The devil with that!" the Rio Kid growled. "I'm goin' in."

He spurred Saber on, fury in his heart. Someone had framed him and he meant to find out who had done it!

CHAPTER
SEVENTEEN

On the Dodge

Not a great while passed at the speed Saber was racing before the Rio Kid saw the work-train, the cars on the siding that served as offices, and the squalid, mud-ruttedd settlement of Junction City ahead on the flats. Smoke hung over the ugly, jerry-built shacks. In the saloons workmen lounged. Or they lay about in the sun, sleeping off the night before.

But Bob Pryor rode straight to the offices of the U.P., threw himself off his horse and hit the steps. He lashed in the door of the car, where he had spoken to George Olliphant, the section assistant. Olliphant sat at his table. He glanced up as the grim-faced Rio Kid stalked to his side.

Olliphant's cold gray eyes fixed on him. The stout, semi-bald man looked frightened for a moment as he saw the Rio Kid, and he made a convulsive movement toward a nearby drawer, but Pryor caught him by the shoulder.

"What in all creation's the meanin' of this, Olliphant?" snarled the Rio Kid, throwing the "Wanted" circular down on the desk.

"Why, I — uh — that is, I —" stammered Olliphant.

A yellow look touched the flesh about his flaccid mouth. His hand shook as he picked up the circular, pretending to read it.

Suspicion flashed through the Rio Kid, but before he could speak again, suddenly he heard the *cluck-cluck* of a cocking shotgun. A young fellow behind him jumped up, training a double-barreled scattergun on Pryor's ribs.

"I'll blow you inside out, Rio Kid, if you move!" he shouted. "Get up your hands."

"Nice work, Harris!" exclaimed Olliphant. "Oh, Marshal — Marshal Hawks! This way, quick!" He leaned out the open window of the car, bellowing loudly for the law.

"Somebody's framed me, Olliphant," the Rio Kid growled, "and I reckon yuh know who it was."

"Keep that gun steady on him, Harris!" Olliphant cried, excited. "He's a killer!"

"You know that I come to yuh and warned yuh of Kane and his crew the day *after* the holdup," Pryor said. "You know I had nothin' to do with that holdup!"

There was a look of triumph in the stout man's cold gray eyes, gloating over the Rio Kid, pinned to the double barrels.

"Kill him if he moves!" he said to Harris.

A big man in whipcord and Stetson, six-shooters at his waist, a railraod detective, came bounding into the car.

"What's up, Boss?" he cried.

"There he is — the Rio Kid," shouted Olliphant. "Arrest him! Take his guns, Hawks."

"Yuh're the Rio Kid, all right," Hawks said, eyeing Pryor closely as he advanced with a menacing hand on his Colt butt. "I've seen yuh around camp. That was a mean job yuh done. Where's the rest of the money? Yuh got it on yuh?"

"That's the man, Hawks," Olliphant said icily. "I can identify him, though he wore a mask. I'd know him anywhere."

"That stickup was done before I come to see yuh, Olliphant," the Rio Kid protested. "Why didn't yuh identify me then?"

Olliphant leaped to his feet, his face, even his bald spot turning scarlet.

"I don't know what he's talking about, Hawks!" he shouted. "He's a murderer and a thief! We found part of the stolen payroll in his bag, and I'll swear he's the bandit!"

"Unbuckle yore gun-belt and drop," Hawks commanded, lifting his pistol.

With clenched fists the Rio Kid had started at Olliphant, who hastily put the table between himself and the man he so falsely accused. A quick glance told Pryor that the men in the car were not the shift who had been here when he had made his previous visit. Anyway, they had had only a brief glimpse of him before Olliphant had taken him outside. They might not recall him.

Outside he heard a big, bearded grader roar:

"Hey, boys, they got the Rio Kid! Fetch a rope, quick! He took our money!"

Track layers, graders, and other workers came flying from shacks, or leaping up from the shade where they had been resting. Olliphant looked pleased as a glance out the window showed him the gathering mob.

"Shall I call in my boys and snake him out, Boss?" Hawks asked.

"No, no, don't endanger your life for scum like this, Hawks," Olliphant replied, with a snarl. "If they take him, it'll only be what he's got coming."

The Rio Kid, with furious anger in his heart, saw a canvas bag he recognized as his own under the assistant's table. It held extra duffle, equipment he did not carry with him when on a run.

"So yuh found some of the payroll money in my bag, Olliphant," he said.

"Yes, you killer!" shouted Olliphant. "You shot that paymaster without any mercy and you'd have killed me, too, if I hadn't been too quick for you . . . Take him out, Marshal!"

Hawks was reaching for the Rio Kid's guns, for Pryor, intent on the perfidious Olliphant, whom he now knew to be an accomplice of Kane, or perhaps even in command of the gang, had not obeyed the order to drop his belt. The mob outside was gathering swiftly, pushing and cursing, yelling for his blood.

Suddenly a cold voice spoke from the end of the car:

"Just stand quiet and don't try no monkey business."

Wild Bill Hickok stood there, his pearl-handled Colts trained on everybody in the car. At the other end stood Buffalo Bill Cody, also armed and ready.

"You fool!" roared Olliphant. "This man's a murderer."

"Cut it out, Hickok," the railroad detective growled.

But Wild Bill was too well known to be disobeyed. Hawks let his gun rattle to the wooden floor of the car, and raised his hands. The young engineer with the shotgun, George Olliphant's innocent dupe, had already hastily discarded his weapon under Cody's prod.

"Make it pronto, Kid," ordered Wild Bill Hickok coolly. His steady eyes fixed the occupants of the car so that each believed the great gunfighter to be giving him his personal attention. "Get goin'," he snapped. "I told yuh not to ride in here, didn't I? This thing is cut-and-dried."

The Rio Kid knew his friend with the thick mustache was right.

"I'll take care of you later, Olliphant," he called back as he ran swiftly up the car.

Wild Bill backed out on the platform and pushed a big fellow, seeking to climb the steps, in the face with his spurred boot. He sent a couple of bullets over the crowd.

"Hey, that's Wild Bill Hickok!" someone yelled, and the men in front suddenly lost interest in pushing. They tried to duck, stepping on the toes of those in the rear.

"Look out for him!" another voice shrilled. "He never misses!"

Celestino Mireles was waiting, the reins of Saber and Hickok's fast mount in his hands, on the opposite side of the cars. The Rio Kid hit the saddle from the step, and the dun stepped daintily over the ties and rails to the level space alongside the right-of-way.

Hickok plugged two bullets into the wooden platform and the mob scattered in every direction. Then Wild Bill leaped on his own mustang and took off after his friends. Buffalo Bill Cody and Ned Buntline were already tearing away.

Bullets and the frustrated yells of the crowd followed them, as the tough citizens of Junction City took heart at this retreat and came swarming around both ends of the train. But the fleet steeds of the five whirled them out of danger as they galloped parallel with the track, eastward from Junction City.

A few miles out they had left pursuit far behind.

Buffalo Bill swore. "A fine pickle we're in now! Every one of us is liable to be mobbed if we go back!"

"Yuh said it, Cody," growled Bill Hickok. "The Kid's too impetuous. He just would go rushin' in there."

"I'm plumb sorry, boys," said the Rio Kid contritely. "But I couldn't let an hombre like this Olliphant accuse me of bein' a killer and a thief without doin' somethin' about it. If yuh say so I'll go back there and face the music."

"Don't be a danged fool," snapped Hickok. "What in tarnation do yuh think we got yuh out of that scrape for?"

"Yeah," chimed in Cody. "They'd string yuh higher'n a kite. I don't care if I don't go back. I'm sick of slaughterin' buffalo for the railroad. What say we all head for Texas till this blows over?"

140

"Gentlemen," drawled Ned Buntline, "I've got a better idea. I have followed you boys from hot point and back to the starting place, and I reckon I have a little right to speak my piece. Do you agree?"

Everybody grinned and nodded.

"I have had the time of my life bumping over your lovely treeless and waterless ocean on a razorback clothes rack called a horse out in these parts," Buntline went on. "I have broken my teeth on biscuits and on beef that eats and tastes like dried old leather. I have drunk to the fill of warm, poisonous-looking water! Indians are very interesting, especially when a hundred of the howling critters are chasing one white man across the desert far from home. However, despite all these singular advantages and the charming society of the direct and impetuous gentlemen who have left the soft spots of civilization one jump ahead of the sheriff, I am beginning to think of home. It's just a foible, of course, but people are like that."

"He's talkin' about somethin,' Cody, but what?" Hickok said to Cody, with a wink.

"This," the writer answered. "Come on East with me and we'll stage a real act to show those dudes there what the Wild West really is like. I'll write the show and we'll all appear together. I'll guarantee you a good time and money to burn. I can already see it: ' "Scouts of the Prairie," by Ned Buntline, Starring Buffalo Bill Cody, Wild Bill Hickok and the Rio Kid!' Why, it'll draw a million!"

Buffalo Bill stared at Hickok.

"Sounds good to me, boys," he cried.

141

Wild Bill nodded, too.

"It'll put in the time till this blows over," he agreed. "I'll go. How about you, Kid?"

But the Rio Kid shook his head.

"I got business westward," he said.

A pair of dark blue eyes drew him. He could not leave now. His friends needed him in Riverside, and Elsa McClean must not be allowed to believe the reports that would be spread about him by Olliphant.

Pleadings were in vain. The Rio Kid had made up his mind. They shook hands and the party split into two groups, Wild Bill Hickok, Buffalo Bill Cody and Ned Buntline shoving their horses straight east toward Omaha and the Missouri, while the Rio Kid with his loyal trail-mate, Celestino Mireles, at his side, turned to ride a wide circle around Junction City and head for Riverside.

He was on the dodge and fair game for any man's gun.

CHAPTER
EIGHTEEN

The Greed of Man

Caged beasts could have been no more ferocious than the man who stalked up and down before Olliphant.

"Where's the Rio Kid?" he demanded, his eyes glowing with a red hate that only death could quench, glinting in the lamplight of the private railway car. "He's balked me at every turn, Olliphant! The Sioux won't fight unless they have a shore thing. I fixed it for 'em and this Rio Kid brought North and Carr in the nick of time to save them fool settlers. Before that, I had 'em moving when he stopped it. And he killed O'Byrne, our best strong-arm man. We haven't much time left and it would all be settled if it wasn't for this Pryor devil. Nobody's seen him for the past five days, since you lost yore chance to arrest him here."

"Now, Boss, don't let this Rio Kid worry you," soothed George Olliphant. "He's through in Nebraska. A fugitive, with a price of two thousand dollars on his head, which I published and circularized in General Dodge's name. Any man who sees the Kid can shoot him and collect the reward. And — I know where he is!"

"Where?" snarled the boss.

Gentleman Dan Kane, looking wan, drawn and bruised, bit his lip, blinking at mention of the Rio Kid, whom he feared with a deadly terror.

"Where is he?" whispered Kane.

"I just had a wire from our agent in Council Bluffs," said Olliphant triumphantly. "He reports that Buffalo Bill Cody, Wild Bill Hickok and that writer fellow Buntline took the train there this evening for the East. No doubt the Rio Kid's with 'em, keeping out of sight. Go to it, Boss, and don't fail again. General Dodge will soon be back here and heaven help us if he finds what we're up to! I've got to take a flying trip to St. Louis to make sure everything's in order for selling. The corrected survey must be posted within two weeks from tomorrow and it can't be changed after that. So we must take what we want."

"I'll do it," promised the cold-voiced Boss. "The fool troops were pullin' out of Riverside when we left. General Carr and Major North couldn't stick in one place forever. They got to patrol the line. I'll get in touch with Spotted Tail again and fix it for the attack."

"I'll see you when I get back, then," Olliphant said. "We'll make a quick clean-up and run for it. Don't forget, I get thirty percent of the gross take. It ought to amount to a couple of million before we're done. Kane and you pay off the men and divvy the balance."

"Kane'll take what I give him." The Boss scowled at the shaken gambler. "The yella coyote had Barringer under his knife and lost his nerve. He lied to me, or I'da done it myself before I met Spotted Tail."

144

Gentleman Kane shriveled under his leader's angry glare. "I — I just couldn't do it in cold blood," he muttered.

"Yuh've lost yore nerve," snarled the Boss.

"Remember, now," warned Olliphant, "this Sioux trouble'll depress land values all through the Mid-west. Buy up everything you can get cheap on option, but get Riverside and the Slanting B Ranch above all. Here's the balance of that payroll money. I planted four hundred dollars of it in the Rio Kid's baggage. Then I gave out those circulars describing him."

The plotters shook hands. Kane and the Boss left the curtained car, that was fitted out with a berth and living arrangements for the crooked railroad man. They mounted their fast horses, red-tipped feathers sticking up from their Stetsons, and started away from Junction City, where they had come for the important conference with Olliphant.

Nothing would deter the Boss from his plan to kill, and to appropriate the lands the criminal syndicate wanted. For profit the murderous combine had concentrated the Sioux against innocent settlers and townsfolk. Six thousand savage red warriors would descend upon his chosen victims . . .

In the meantime, the Rio Kid and Mireles had crossed the Platte and kept on south. They hid in the brakes along the creeks throughout the daylight hours, getting much needed sleep and rest. They had plenty of food, for their accurate rifles could bring down a buffalo or antelope when desired.

Working toward Riverside, but off the Overland Trail and away from the usual haunts of the Sioux raiders, it was days before the little Frontier town was sighted. The wagons of the emigrants still stood in the square, but Carr's troops and North's Pawnee scouts were gone, hunting their red enemies who were as elusive as shifting clouds.

The trail-mates waited until night fell and yellow candle and lamplight flickered in the windows. A red fire was burning in the square, where the Irish folks were camped.

Then, with the faithful Mireles riding a few feet behind Saber, the Rio Kid made his way into Riverside. He dismounted out from the firelight. McClean's friends were sitting in a circle around the warming blaze, for the September night was cool. They had finished their supper and the men were smoking. Low voices were speaking of the old sod from which these men had so recently come. The Indian uprising had prevented them from settling in the new country, and they were homesick.

The Rio Kid did not see Elsa McClean although her father was squatted on the ground, the ruby glow from the burning buffalo chips lighting up his lined, ruddy countenance. Jim Barringer wasn't present, either. Pryor walked quietly over to the wagon in which Jim had been placed after the Kid had carried him from the flaming building. He heard Elsa's musical tones and his heart leaped. When he went to the back of the wagon she was sitting there, dangling her feet over the dropped

146

tail-boards, while Jim Barringer lay under his blanket inside.

"Bob!" Elsa cried as she recognized his lithe figure standing before her.

"Good evenin'." The Rio Kid smiled at her. "Yuh seem surprised to see me, Elsa. I told yuh I'd be back."

She seized his hand, pressing it nervously.

"You shouldn't have come here!" she cried tensely.

"Why not?"

"You know as well as I do," she said anxiously. "They've got papers posted for you, dead or alive!"

"Yuh don't believe what they're saying about me, do you, Elsa?" he asked softly.

She looked straight into his eyes. "Of course I don't, Bob."

"Me neither," Barringer growled. He reached out his hand, and shook the Rio Kid's.

"How are yuh, Jim?"

"Fine," Barringer said.

"No, he's not, not yet, but he will be," Elsa put in. "He's been dragged through the rake, Bob, and that's the truth. You get in there and keep out of sight till I fetch Dad."

She jumped down and went over to the gathering about the fire. The Rio Kid sat down near Barringer whose face was white in the faint light.

"I'm glad to see yuh, Bob, though what Elsa says is true," Jim told him. "There's men here who would sell their own brother for two thousand dollars. Lots of folks don't know yuh the way I do."

Elsa came back, her father with her.

"By all the saints, Bob, why did ye come here?" exclaimed McClean, seizing his hand.

"I wanted to make shore you folks are all right," replied the Rio Kid. "None of yore folks would turn me up for the reward money, would they?"

"No, no, Bob. But there's men say they'll shoot ye on sight and collect the reward the railroad's put up. They say you kilt a man in cold blood and stole a fortune."

"They believe it?"

"Those who don't know you do. I don't, and never will, not even if ye sat there yerself and insisted on it!"

"Thanks."

"But this is no place for ye, my boy. Nor any town hereabouts. Men will kill ye for that blood money."

"And you needn't put your neck in danger for us again, Bob," said Elsa earnestly. "The soldiers say they'll hunt down the Indians, and that they seldom hit twice in the same spot. We won't stir from here, where we're safe, till the land's pacified."

The pale light touched the rugged jaw of the Rio Kid, the glow of his eyes showing his fearlessness, his confidence. No panic touched his heart. His Stetson chin-strap drew up his strong jaw, and his lithe figure was fully at ease.

"Elsa," he said quietly, "I got something to tell yuh. Will yuh walk over by the river with me?"

"Yes, Bob. Father, you stay here with Jim."

The Rio Kid saw Barringer's white face watching him from his sick bed. But Jim Barringer did not say anything as the girl he loved went away with his rival.

148

A slice of moon was touching the far horizon, sending a silver streak across the dark waters of the river. The bluffs were black as ink in the shadows across the stream.

The Rio Kid took the girl's hand.

"Elsa," he said, "I want yuh to come away with me — marry me."

Her breath was a sob as she looked up into his eyes. "I can't, Bob."

"Because of what's happened?"

"You know it isn't that," she said, injured to the quick. "I'd follow you anywhere, Bob, if I could."

"I shouldn'ta said that, Elsa. I know yuh would. Why won't you come? Is it Barringer?"

"Yes," she said.

He was silent for a moment. Then he said:

"You hate this flat country, Elsa, but Jim was born to it and he'll stay here. Yuh'll live in a soddy on the plains. Come to the Pecos with me, to the mountains. It's wild but there's nothin' as beautiful."

Elsa began crying, softly. The Rio Kid put his arm about her and held her.

"Don't!" he begged. "I won't say any more."

"You should have seen his eyes when father told him of what the Indians had done to his mother and sister," she sobbed. "He didn't say a word — nothing at all. It was horrible. He's alone in the world and he's only a boy. I can't leave him. I'm all he has to cling to now."

"And me?" se asked, smiling at her.

"You're strong, Bob. You'll always be strong. Even with every man's hand turned against you now you're not afraid. You're the best man I've ever known and I wish I could tell you how much I admire you. I'd go with you tonight if it weren't for Jim. What you say is true. I don't like it here and I fear the savages. But I've got to stay. You believe me, don't you?"

"Yes, Elsa, I do. I knew you were like that, and that's why I tried so hard to get you."

He kissed her lips and she held to him for a time.

"General! Pronto! Zere ees no time to lose!"

Mireles was hurrying up with the horses. A shout sounded from the square and lanterns flickered, waving toward the river where Bob Pryor stood.

"Someone saw us on ze way een, General!" said Mireles. "Ze mob comes! Pronto! Mount and ride!"

"Go — go on, Bob!" Elsa cried. "Hurry!"

The Rio Kid looked toward the approaching citizens. He saw the mayor of Riverside, the portly Phil Harris, with a shotgun in one hand and a lantern in the other, and Warren Grebe, the hotel-keeper, with Colts strapped about his waist. There were other men of the town which he had saved from the torch and tomahawk of the Sioux. Thirty or forty were coming to seize him, whipped up by the big reward posted for him.

"There he is — over there." Grebe shouted.

"There's the Rio Kid, boys!" Mayor Harris echoed. "Arrest him!"

A couple of wild bullets sang over Pryor's head. He pushed Elsa quickly toward her wagon.

"Run, Elsa!"

"Good-by, Bob!" she sobbed. "And good luck!"

150

She kissed him again, then started to run toward the fire.

The Rio Kid seized Saber's reins and mounted, Mireles impatiently dancing his wild mustang close at hand.

"Come, General! Zey have us against ze rivaire!"

Bullets and howls were coming thicker and closer.

"Circle around there, and cut 'em off!" bellowed Mayor Harris, then horsemen were swinging into wide arcs to trap the fugitive.

Contempt was in the Rio Kid's heart. Then he saw McClean, Riley and others of the emigrants rush out, guns in hand. They meant to help him, and he could not allow this. Nor would he injure the misguided denizens of Riverside.

Whirling the dun, he put Saber straight down the bank into the water. Mireles followed. Out of depth, the horses began to swim. On the other side a deep cut in the bluffs showed a gentle incline up to the plateau level.

The two fleeing men, follwed by bullets from those they had saved from death, hit the upswing.

CHAPTER
NINETEEN

The Rio Kid's Debut

I reckon that'll be Dogtooth Gap," the Rio Kid said to his trail-mate, Celestino Mireles.

"*Si* Ees wider zan ze gap at Rivairside, General. Pair-haps ze railroad come here affair all."

"Huh. Mebbe. Noboddy but General Dodge and a few insiders know yet."

They found an easy place down to the water and Mireles shoved his mustang into the stream. But hardly had the animal taken three steps before the Mexican uttered a sharp cry and floundered off the sinking beast's back. The horse was up to his belly in whirling sand, sinking fast.

"Quicksand!" cried Pryor, ripping Saber back in the nick of time.

His lariat whipped from its hook and with a quick twirl he threw to Mireles, who caught it and was pulled to the shore.

Dismounting, the Rio Kid set about helping rescue the snorting, maddening mustang in the deadly grip of the shifting sands, now closing over his rear quarters. The strong rawhide circled the animal's neck, and the two men pulled with all their might, nearly choking the mustang. However, with this help he managed to extricate himself and drag out on the firmer footing, covered with muck and shaking with terror.

Celestino washed him down, then he and the Rio Kid mounted and went back up on the plain. Across the river they could see the new townsite where Chickenhead Sims, with a couple of dozen other citizens had begun throwing up soddies and tents. The raw settlement looked uninviting, and when Sims shouted at them and picked up a rifle the Rio Kid shrugged.

"I reckon the news has got down here," he drawled. "And I reckon we can get along without seein' any more of Dogtooth Gap."

"Where we go, General?" Mireles asked.

"I'm thinkin' of headin' for the real East. Buffalo Bill and Ned Buntline are good sports. A turn with 'em wouldn't hurt me."

He hid the bitter disappointment in his heart. But he wanted to get away from the Frontier for a time.

It was a week later when he took his leave of Mireles, on the west bank of the Missouri.

"Take care of Saber, Celestino," he said, and wait here for me. I'll be back when I'm back."

"*Si*, General."

The dark eyes of the Mexican were sad, but he would obey.

Spruced up in fresh clothing and with money in his jeans, the Rio Kid boarded a train that sped him away from the plains. Forty-eight hours later he walked into the hotel in St. Louis where Buffalo Bill Cody, Wild Bill

Hickok and Ned Buntline were staying. Flaming posters advertising Buntline's new play "Scouts of the Prairie" at the city theater were plastered all over the town, and inquiry had sent Pryor to his friends.

Knocking on the door of the suite, a gruff voice called, "Come in!" The Rio Kid stepped in, and recoiled in mock horror as he saw the plumes of his partner, Buffalo Bill. Cody was in elegant store clothes. Hickok, too, was elegantly attired in light-blue, swallow-tailed coat and tight-fitting new pants. Buntline wore trousers and shirt, and his brown hair was rumpled. Pens and a bottle of ink, piles of paper were on the table before him.

"Bob!" cried Cody. "C'mon in! Help yoreself to the whiskey and seegars over there. Glad to see yuh. We're rehearsin'."

Buffalo Bill looked a little ashamed of himself as the Rio Kid took a chair and tried to hide his grins while the famous scout declaimed the florid lines ripped off by the swift Buntline pen.

"'Unhand that woman!'" roared Cody, in a voice that would have carried over a tornado. "'Yuh red devil, yuh've come tothe end of yore trail!'"

"*Bang!*" shouted Buntline. "That's where you shoot, Bill."

Buffalo Bill grinned. "Laugh if yuh want, Kid. I know I'm an awful actor. However, I like it. It suits me to a T. We tried out last night and it went fine."

"We'll make plenty," Buntline told them. "How about it, Pryor? Will you join the act? Too late to put

154

your name on the bills this week but when we hit Chicago I'll have some new ones printed."

"Anything for a laugh," agreed the Rio Kid. "If they can stomach Cody I reckon they can stand to look at me, too."

It was good to be with his friends, and in new surroundings. A veteran soldier and a great traveler, the Rio Kid knew that time alone would heal the wound in his heart from losing Elsa McClean. He would plunge into this new life and make the most of it.

They practiced Buntline's heroic lines and scenes all through the afternoon, snatched a bite together at a restaurant, then went to the theater in a cab. Some extras had been hired to rush on, attired as Indians, shooting blanks, and it was up to Buffalo Bill, Hickok, Buntline and the Rio Kid to save the settler's home from the savages.

The Rio Kid stood in the wings watching the opening scene. He was not to come on until the next. It was crude drama, but the city audience loved it, especially when the guns roared and Indians bit the dust. Applause and laughter were loud, and there was no doubt that Buffalo Bill and his show would be a great hit.

Buntline, with sweat streaming down his painted cheeks from the heat of the oil-lamp footlights, took off his Stetson and bowed to the audience at the end of the first scene.

"And now, Ladies and Gents," the author announced, "I have a special surprise for you. A great friend of mine and one of the most famous frontiersmen of the

West is here with us tonight, a man whose unerring Colt has downed the worst bad men from the Texas to Dakota. Ladies and Gentlemen, I present to you the well known Rio Kid!"

It was Bob Pryor's first appearance as an actor, and he was blinded for a moment by the lights as he stepped out beside Buntline and stared at the blurred sea of smiling faces before him. He felt he was all hands and feet but he had been on parade in the Army and knew how to carry himself. The stage fright passed and he came to attention and saluted, laughing, and the audience began to cheer and clap.

"We will now go on with the show," said Buntline. "In the next scene our heroine is left alone by her father, who had to drive to town to get himself a fresh supply of mountain dew, and the Indians attack the cabin. Watch closely now."

There was a stir in a stage box, close to the Rio Kid's right as he stood by the upstage wing. His eyes had grown accustomed to the foots and he saw the man who had risen from his gilt chair in the box.

"Olliphant!" Pryor roared, at sight of the stout engineer, who had framed him with a murder and robbery charge, made him a fugitive from justice with a price on his head.

Olliphant wore elegant evening dress and he was with another man and two painted ladies. He had been drinking heavily, and his round face and bald head were red.

"That fellow's wanted for murder!" he shrieked, pointing at the Rio Kid, who was starting his way.

Olliphant had not been aware that Pryor was in the play. Perhaps he had come with malice in his heart against Cody and Hickok, meaning to make trouble for them. But the sight of the Rio Kid had startled him, even though he had believed the man he had injured was with the others in hiding.

The Rio Kid wore a double belt with two large six-shooters in the holsters. They were loaded with blanks, of course, for the show. He whipped one and fired point-blank at Olliphant who screamed and cowered in the box. The audience began to laugh, believing it part of the performance as the Rio Kid jumped the footlights, stepped on the rail of the box, and launched himself upon the fat engineer.

The two painted girls fled from the box screaming, and Olliphant's male companion dived over the side. Pryor smashed his fists into Olliphant's flabby flesh, broke his lip against his teeth, bloodied his nose and blacked his eyes.

"Po-lice! Po-lice!" Olliphant was yelling shrilly.

Shouts were going up now, as people realized that this was no part of the performance, but in eanest. Uniformed police officers, in high helmets, were starting down the side aisle, and the whole hall roared with confusion and alarm. Suddenly someone seized Pryor by the shoulders and ripped him off the prostrate, whimpering Olliphant, whose face was a gory mess.

"Yuh fool, Bob!" cried Buffalo Bill. "Look out — here comes the police!"

Hickok and Buntline seized his arms, and the three practically threw him back onto the stage and rushed him out through the stage door.

"Run for it, Bob!" ordered Buntline. "Don't go to the hotel yet. Meet us there at midnight."

Pryor ran from the back exit and just managed to elude the officers after him. He wandered off through the city, waiting until it was time to meet his friends at the hotel. Cody finally met him and piloted him to the rear of the hotel.

"The police have a man watchin' for yuh in the lobby," growled Cody. "Hafta sneak in through the basement."

Up in the suite, Buntline got up from his writing and surveyed the Rio Kid ruefully.

"A fine actor you turned out to be," he accused. "Not that it hurt the show any. In fact, the publicity'll be wonderful. But they've got a warrant out for you, and Olliphant's howling for your arrest. You'll have to hide. Do you need money?"

"No." Pryor grinned. "I've got plenty, Ned. I reckon I don't belong in the city, gents. I'll head back for the Frontier."

He noted the title of Buntline's newest story, "The Rio Kid's Revenge."

"Well, be careful they don't pick yuh up on that killin'," warned Wild Bill.

Pryor shook hands all around, said good-by, and left by the basement eluding the watching policeman in the lobby . . .

Celestino Mireles was delighted to see him a day later, gripping his hand warmly.

"Saber ees act like ba-bee for you, General," he cried.

Celestino had slept at the livery stable with the horses. The Rio Kid went into the stall, and the dun whimpered, nosing his master's hand, rolling his eyes.

"What we do, General?" inquired Mires. 'We go to Tej-as?"

"Nope," the Rio Kid growled. "I'm through runnin'. I'm goin' to find Gentleman Dan Kane, Celestino, and beat the truth out of him. I'll clear my name or know the reason why."

They headed west in the dawn, paralleling the Union Pacific tracks. But as they left the eastern part of Nebraska, they found the outlying stations and settlements in a state of paralyzed fear. The Sioux were striking with full fury along the line, and beyond.

Nothing had ever been known like the Red Terror which gripped the Frontier, as Spotted Tail, Sitting Bull, Gall and Crazy Horse rose to heights of devilish attack. Men dared not ride without a strong escort, and the railroad builders had been checked. Brave as they were, they could work only with a regiment of cavalry watching every instant, for the Indians would creep close in at night, hide in a swale, be on them and kill and away within minutes.

Pryor sent Mireles in to Junction City to spy around for signs of Kane. The Mexican was a genius at ferreting out information. In his dark clothing, with wide sombrero pulled low, he looked like any other Mexican and drew little attention.

But Celestino returned to him with word that Kane had gone westward and had not been seen for three days at the camp.

"Mebbe they figger this is the time to strike Riverside," murmured the Rio Kid. "I s'pose Carr and North had to leave. Anyway, I'm goin' to hunt up Kane, and there's another hombre I mean to check on, too. I bin thinkin' it over and the more I think, the fishier he looks. C'mon!"

CHAPTER
TWENTY

The Field of Battle

Long hours the two rode at night, always fully alert, pushing on for the Wood River. They saw many small bands of Indians in the distance but avoided clashes, as the Rio Kid's scouting ability shielded them from danger. Both wore a red-tipped eagle feather in case the dodge might work again if they ran into Sioux warriors, although Pryor was too shrewd not to realize that many of the Indians now knew him on sight.

"The Brule are warned 'bout me by this time, anyways," he told his friend.

They waited for the sun to drop behind the bluffs, and in the dark of the new night Bob Pryor and his lithe partner slid into Riverside, shadows in the shadows. Watching, flat on his belly, after a long wait the Rio Kid touched Mireles' wrist.

"There's Kane — and that hunch of mine was right. Look who's with him! Get back. They're ridin' out."

Like wraiths they faded away as half a dozen riders passed along the alley and pushed south out of Riverside. Then the Rio Kid, allowing them a start, took up their trail.

An hour's run, and they came to country broken by buttes and the ravine of a small rill that joined the Wood River. The white renegades were met here by Indians who treated them as friends, thus cinching the Rio Kid's suspicions.

In the stir Pryor, who had dismounted and crept in on foot, was able to get up close enough to see the red fire glows in the swale below. He heard the stampings of hundreds of mustangs, with a low sound now and then which told him he had located a big concealed Indian camp.

Kane and his mates stayed for two hours in the Sioux encampment, then returned to Riverside. They went to their living quarters, while the Rio Kid flitted in the rear of the building which stood close to the house in which Barringer had been held a prisoner.

Gentleman Dan Kane, he discovered, slept in a small side room which gave out on the alley. Under the bottom edge of the sash, Pryor watched the gambler remove his black coat, pull off his spurred black boots with a grunt and he down on the cot, blowing out the candle.

After a time Kane began snoring. Pryor softly pushed up the window inch by inch, until he could squeeze his body through.

Standing over the sleeping gambler, he put one hand over Kane's lips and with the other held a pistol against the man's breast, putting all his weight on him to keep him from starting up.

Startled awake, Kane struggled but the Rio Kid said menacingly in his ear:

"If yuh don't lie quiet, Kane, I'll blow yore insides out!"

Gentleman Dan stopped struggling and his eyes glowed with fear in the dimness.

"I can take yuh any time I want, Dan," went on Pryor, his voice low. "But I'll give yuh one chance to square yoreself. I savvy yuh're not at the head of this dirty business, and I'll name yore Boss for yuh so's yuh'll see I know what's up."

He whispered a name in Kane's ear. That clinched it for Gentleman Dan. Shivering, he gave in completely.

"I knew you'd come up with me, Rio Kid," he whispered hoarsely. "I thought of running away."

"I'd foller yuh to the hot place," the Rio Kid said grimly. "On the other hand, I'll see yuh git off mighty light if yuh help me clear myself and take yore Boss right."

Kane's nerve was not turned to such dangerous business as he had been forced. It had stretched and snapped long before, and the Rio Kid was his bugaboo. O'Byrne's death, the might of Pryor, and his inside knowledge of the gang's workings combined to break him.

"All right," Kane promised. "I — I'll do what you say, Kid, if only you'll give me a break . . ."

Reveille was sounding in the army camp as the Rio Kid on the lathered dun dashed into the company street. This was General Eugene A. Carr's division, the Fifth Cavalry and the associated battalion of Major Frank North's Pawnee scouts. With them were all the necessary field accoutrements and supplies. Big blue army wagons stood, filled with duffel and food for the troopers.

"Howdy, Major," sang out the Rio Kid.

He had ridden for hours to reach the camp. The sentries had let him through after he had identified himself. Dismounting, he seized the surprised North's hand and pumped his arm.

"Look here, Bob," North said worriedly, "there's a warrant out for you, dead or alive, for that U.P. robbery. This is no place for you to be. My duty is to put you under arrest. Carr will see to it if I don't. Jump on your horse and run for it."

"Forget it, Frank, till our work's done," Pryor smiled. "Then yuh can arrest me and Carr can too. I'll clear up that charge that was framed on me. But we've got to work fast. Three thousand Sioux are goin' to strike Riverside just 'fore dawn tomorrer and wipe the whole place out!"

"What — again?" exclaimed North.

"Yeah, that's the center of what they're after, and white men I can name for yuh are eggin' the Indians on. I can lead yuh to their hide-out and if we leave the baggage behind, we can make it in the nick."

North's eyes lighted up. "It isn't Spotted Tail's gang, is it?"

"Yes, suh."

"All the better. We've been after that red ghost for weeks! Wait'll I tell General Carr."

"Hustle, Frank. We ain't got any time to waste."

164

He began rubbing down Saber, giving the dun a drink and a light feed. Then he begged breakfast from the army cook, and had hardly finished when General Carr sent for him. Men in the company streets were already saddling their horses to the bugles, preparing to ride.

Carr and North led the procession. The Rio Kid rode with them for a time, then joined the out-riding advance scouts, Pawnees smelling the way. All through the day they marched, following the ragged lines of timber that grew along the stream beds.

The cavalrymen were pining for a real blow against the Sioux, so elusive, so difficult to come up with. Bob Pryor was offering it to them. At dusk they paused for a drink and a cold bite.

Guns, pistols, and Spencer carbines were checked on order, and extra ammunition, brought by horsepack, issued to the troops.

Orders were given by word of mouth, passed from Carr and North through the subalterns and sergeants to the line.

In the night they resumed the forced march. The Rio Kid knew the Sioux too well to hope for a complete surprise, but during the ride he had talked over the strategy with General Carr and North and his plan was followed.

Well out from possible Indian sentries, the command split into three columns. Major North's Pawnees, with the Rio Kid, were to creep ahead, line along the Wood River, and close in from that direction. Two semicircular columns, one to the north and the other to the south of the ravine where the Rio Kid had located the Brule camp, were stabbing ahead in the darkness, pincering in so there would be no escape when they jumped the foe.

Because of the projected raid on Riverside, the Sioux would have their braves pulled in, and be ready to ride off once their horrible job was done. And they would not be expecting a counter-attack.

The west wind which blew in their faces was a factor which Bob Pryor counted on to help the surprise. With the Pawnees, who could move with the stealth of animals, he cut up to the west of the swale. The stars twinkled bright overhead. The moon was rising beyond. In the distance he could see a faint red glow over the Indian camp as they stole in. Then, in position, they waited.

North was close to the Rio Kid and the big Pawnees, with Spencers and scalping knives ready.

"Is it time yet?" whispered Pryor.

They could hear faint sounds of stirring in the enemy camp below. North looked at his watch, for the attack had been timed to coincide with that of the other two columns.

"Three forty-two," North breathed.

"Let's get in, then! Carr's buglers ought to sound in a minute."

They were up, rushing in, still silent. Then Carr's bugles suddenly pierced the cool air as the Sioux, making ready to strike at Riverside, found themselves in turn surprised.

166

As the bugles sounded the charge, the Pawnees began to whoop. Gunfire began as the Sioux sprang to arms. From every direction the Indians found their foes, every one an expert marksman hot for revenge.

Terrifying whoops rang out. The Sioux were brave and lashed back, grabbing their mustangs and riding out of the trap, but only to be met by the disciplined troops. The melee was terrific for minutes that dragged like hours. The cold gray light of dawn cast a nightmare illumination over the field of battle.

Spotted Tail, leading his braves, rode up against the lines of dismounted troopers, personally commanded by General Carr. The Pawnees, shooting, stabbing, were pressing them in. Knives flashed, and scalps ripped loose.

Torn to pieces by the volleys of the repeating Spencers, the Sioux fell back into the ravine, but the Pawnees were waiting for them in the brush. Hand-to-hand encounters took place. The screams of wounded men and horses, the clang of arms lifted in the morning air, as the fight went on.

The Rio Kid was in the thick of it, on his dun. Saber was in his glory, loving a scrap as he did. Sioux were breaking through, here and there, by sheer weight of numbers. But the attackers had the advantage of surprise and position and Spotted Tail sought in vain to rally his full force for a counter-blow.

Major North's tall figure dominated the scene. He fought with an icy fury that never permitted a strategic error. The Pawnees, naked and painted, knives bloody, slashed in and out at their hereditary enemies.

The battle raged for an hour in full force as the sun climbed up in the sky. On a small crest, General Carr, Major North and the Rio Kid crouched, looking over the broken stretch where the Sioux were defending themselves, and taking stock of the strategic situation.

"It's going well, gentlemen," Carr remarked. "How many do you figure leaked through, Major?"

"Oh, perhaps fifty per cent," North replied. "But it's an awful blow to the Brules and their allies. They'll take to the tall timber after this!"

Bullets were flying over them, and some cut the ground. A horseman came spurring up to their position, a civilian by his clothing. His fast mustang was covered with dust and sweat. As he appeared the Rio Kid rose up to see who it was.

"Get down, mister," he warned, taking in the keen-faced young man who threw himself from his worn horse. "Lead's mighty thick around these parts. Who are yuh, anyway?"

"My name's Stanley — Henry M. Stanley. I'm a reporter for the New York *Herald*. There's a big battle going on, I take it?"

"That's what it sounds like," Pryor grinned.

"Where's General Carr? Is Major North here? How many Sioux have you got down in that ravine? How long have you been fighting?"

He saw the general's gold epaulets then, and pushed up to the crest beside Carr and North.

The Rio Kid, reloading, took a drink from his canteen. He had come out for a brief breathing spell. Blood spattered him, but most of it came from his enemies. He was not seriously hurt, and was about ready to plunge back into the melee.

"Why, good morning, Mr. Stanley," he heard Carr say, with a laugh. "Always on hand where the fighting's thickest, as usual. I've got a good story for you, or will have, once we finish with those red fellows down there."

Henry Morton Stanley, in his first flare as an ace reporter, was covering the Sioux war for his new employer, James Gordon Bennett, founder of the *Herald*. Stanley's greatest exploit was still to come — the finding of teh missionary-explorer, David Livinstone, in the heart of equatorial Africa, when Stanley made the famous remark, "Doctor Livingstone, I presume?"

Already Stanley showed his genius for ferreting out news. He had arrived on the spot as the battle raged, through a combination of luck and a keen instinct for where the story would break.

The Pawnees were whooping it up, a new note in their savage voices. The Rio Kid ran back, leaped on Saber, and tore down into the thick of the fight. He found several of his big red allies shooting at a bunch of men who were hidden in a hollow.

"White men," Big Bear told him.

The Rio Kid glanced over the rock behind which they crouched. A Stetson rose, a Stetson with a red-tipped eagle feather in it, as the owner fired a Colt at them.

"They're Sioux just the same, Big Bear," the Rio Kid growled. "Take 'em all. Yuh can treat 'em like Dakotas."

These men were the remnant of the gang he was after. Presently the Pawnees dashed in, sweeping over them. Tomahawks flashed crimson in the air!

CHAPTER
TWENTY-ONE

The Boss

Gunfire was dying off, for the Sioux had broken through and ridden away in disordered retreat, or lay dead or circled as prisoners in the ravine. The Pawnees were having a field day, and the Rio Kid, tired of the bloody battle which had reached its final stage, rode the sweated dun out of the swale and approached General Carr and Major North.

Several more men had come up, and among them Pryor recognized one man in dusty riding clothes, a man with thick curly hair on a massive head and shrewd, deep-set eyes. He was the great railroad engineer, General Grenville Dodge, in charge of the Union Pacific.

"This is one bunch of Sioux that won't bother your railroad builders for awhile, Dodge," Carr remarked with a grim smile.

"I was looking for you, Carr," Dodge growled. "The situation's got so bad something had to be done about it. Construction must go on but the Sioux have us about stopped. Perhaps this will be a lesson to 'em."

The Rio Kid knew Dodge, and admired him as did everyone who knew the splendid engineer and fighting man whose genius had made the transcontinental railroad possible, joining the Atlantic and Pacific and uniting the nation.

"We're about finished, I reckon," said Major North.

"No, there's one thing more, gents," drawled the Rio Kid. "And I see it comin'!"

A large band of riders from Riverside approached the crest. Among them the Rio Kid recognized some of his Irish friends, the mayor of the town, and Warren Grebe, the hotelkeeper. And Gentleman Dan Kane was tagging along at the rear of the procession on a black horse.

Pryor was covered with grime and blood from the long battle, but Grebe recognized him and spurred forward.

"That's the Rio Kid, boys!" he howled. "Don't let him get away this time! String him up where he belongs, the dirty murderer!"

"The Rio Kid!" exclaimed General Dodge, looking closely at Pryor. "Why, so it is! Pryor, you're wanted for killing my paymaster and stealing the week's payroll! Seize him, men!"

"Just a sec," the Rio Kid said coolly. "Kane, step up here and speak yore piece."

Gentleman Dan gulped, went yellow about the gills, shot a glance sideward but he was more afraid of Bob Pryor than of anything else. He dismounted and came over, taking a position of safety behind the Rio Kid before he spoke.

"The Rio Kid's innocent," he said. "George Olliphant sold out, General Dodge, and Olliphant shot that paymaster and stole the money. That's nothing. The Boss of all the devilment, the man who planned it and brought Olliphant in, is right there!"

Accusingly Kane pointed straight at Warren Grebe, the Riverside hotel man.

"Why, yuh doublecrossing liar!" exploded Grebe.

"Keep him off me, Rio Kid," Kane screamed, shrinking back. "He did it to get Riverside and the Slanting B, and all the land he could! Olliphant knew the right-of-way was coming through here and that car shops are to be built near town. Grebe enlisted Spotted Tail and the Sioux. I didn't want to sic the red devils on women and kids!"

"Hold it, Grebe!" roared Pryor.

The maddened Boss, whose evil brain had planned the worst excesses of death for the innocent, had whipped a revolver from inside his shirt. His first shot drilled a hole in the Rio Kid's Stetson crown as Bob crouching, drew his own hot Colt. The murderous Grebe's bullet cut a bit from Kane's thickened ear, and Gentleman Dan fell down, yelling for help. On the echo, the Rio Kid's pistol bellowed its direct reply at Grebe, who had jerked his reins, to run for it. The slug hit Grebe just below the temple as the man was in the act of pulling his trigger. As the Rio Kid's bullet struck him, the weight of his gun brought down his arm and his final slug plugged into dirt between Pryor's spread boots.

The mustang bounded forward and the relaxing knees let go. Warren Grebe fell and rolled to a final stop.

172

Frozen silence held the group for a moment. Then the Rio Kid, letting his six-gun slip back into its supple holster, broke the stillness.

"Grebe sicked the Sioux on Riverside, gents. First he tried to get the folks there to move by holdin' Dogtooth Gap out as a bait. But the river's full of quicksands down there and the gap through the bluffs ain't as good as here. Grebe worked in with Olliphant, and forced Kane into the game.

"It took time for me to get on to Grebe. He was mighty cunnin'. 'Twasn't till I thought over that wound he claimed he got, after he done tricked Jim Barringer into his hotel that day so's the gang could capture Jim, that I got really leery of Grebe. No Sioux would ride off and leave a white man the way Grebe claimed. 'Twas just a straw but it started me thinkin' right, and other things fitted in. Actually, Grebe was creased by a bullet from our side in the big battle. He covered it by purtendin' the Sioux done it, settin' hisself in Carr's way to be picked up.

"From now on, Riverside'll be safe. Spotted Tail's goin' to think twice 'fore he visits these parts again, now that Grebe won't be sickin' the Indians on the town. And in a few months the Union Pacific'll be along. Those who hold in Riverside'll be rich. I reckon the Slantin' B, where Kane claims the railroad means to build its shops, ought to be worth plenty, too."

General Dodge came over and held out his hand.

"I'm mighty glad to know you're not guilty, Pryor. I'll see to it that Olliphant's fully punished for what he's done. He'll hang for that murder. Any reward goes to you, of course."

"Never mind that, General," replied the Rio Kid. "I'll ask just one thing."

"And that?"

"A break for Dan Kane. I promised it to him for helpin' me, and he told me the whole story about Grebe and the Sioux bein' here where we could strike 'em. I'd smell the Sioux out, but Kane was quite a help. Yuh'll need Kane till yuh've prosecuted Olliphant. After that I want yuh to let him off easy. He ain't the killer type at all. Grebe had him scared."

"Granted," Dodge promised. "I'll make sure Kane's let off when we're through."

Pryor swung around and helped Kane up. "Yuh heard what the General says, Dan. Never let me run into yuh agin hooked up to a crooked game, savvy?"

"Thanks, Rio Kid," the gambler said whole-heartedly.

"I'm through with devils like Grebe."

A glad cry rang in Pryor's ear, then Michael McClean had seized his hand and was wringing it.

"Bob! Ye're a sight for sore eyes. So ye're all right now. They're sayin' you didn't kill that feller after all. Come over to camp. Elsa and Jim'll be happy to see you."

The Rio Kid smiled and shook his head. "I'll be glad to visit yuh one of these days, Mike — Elsa and Jim and you. There's no more special danger from the Sioux around here for yuh, and yuh can settle down as yuh've a mind to. Good luck."

"I wish you'd come, Bob," begged McClean.

"No, Mike. I've got to be ridin'. I'm headin' south."

The Rio Kid and his faithful comrade, Celestino Mireles, paused only to spruce up, and to have a quick bite.

Then they mounted and struck out over the great plains, running south. The railroad was coming and with it the civilized world with its blessings — and its taints as well.

It was as Elsa McClean had said — the Rio Kid was strong and nothing could dim his power. He rode with his chin up, a mighty soul alone, headed for the wilds, for exciting spots on the Frontier, steady as Fate.